THE BAD MAN

A Novel

CHARLES HANSON TOWNE

Based on the Play by Porter Emerson Browne

The Bad Man

Charles Hanson Towne

© 1st World Library – Literary Society, 2005
PO Box 2211
Fairfield, IA 52556
www.1stworldlibrary.org
First Edition

LCCN: 2006902688

Softcover ISBN: 1-4218-1821-3
Hardcover ISBN: 1-4218-1721-7
eBook ISBN: 1-4218-1921-X

Purchase *"The Bad Man"*
as a traditional bound book at:
www.1stWorldLibrary.org/purchase.asp?ISBN=1-4218-1821-3

1st World Library Literary Society is a nonprofit
organization dedicated to promoting literacy by:

- Creating a free internet library accessible from any
  computer worldwide.
- Hosting writing competitions and offering book
  publishing scholarships.

The Bad Man
contributed by Tim, Ed & Rodney
in support of
1st World Library Literary Society

To

HOLBROOK BLINN

CONTENTS

CHAPTER I. 11

Wherein it is shown that a young American had the courage to come into a new country; how fate played against him, and a neighbor looked longingly at his ranch.

CHAPTER II. 16

Wherein, far away, another man hears whispers of the wealth along the border, and comes down to see about it.

CHAPTER III..30

Wherein Uncle Henry speaks his mind - as usual.

CHAPTER IV...45

Wherein "Red" reveals his heart, and Mrs. Quinn gives him good coffee and good advice.

CHAPTER V. 52

Wherein Gilbert Jones is worried, and Lucia Pell is asked to do an impossible thing.

CHAPTER VI..64

Wherein an old love awakens, Pell reveals his true colors, a mortgage is about to be foreclosed, the contents of a satchel are made known, Uncle Henry springs a sensation, and Pell takes an option.

CHAPTER VII. 103

Wherein Lucia sees treachery brewing, Pell proves himself a brute, and an unexpected guest appears.

CHAPTER VIII. 112

Wherein the bandit expounds a new philosophy, and makes marionettes of the Americans.

CHAPTER IX. 126

Wherein Uncle Henry chatters some more, there is an auction, and things look black indeed.

CHAPTER X. 139

Wherein an old friendship comes to life, Lopez learns a thing or two, and finally makes a match.

CHAPTER XI. 162

Wherein a man proves himself a craven, a shot rings out, and the bad man explains one little hour.

CHAPTER XII. 170

Wherein the bad man cannot understand the good man, and disappears; and a dead man stirs.

CHAPTER XIII. 190

Wherein an old situation seems about to be repeated, another shot is fired, and the bad man comes back.

CHAPTER XIV. 209

Wherein an old friend returns, and there is a joyful reunion.

CHAPTER I

WHEREIN IT IS SHOWN THAT A YOUNG AMERICAN HAD THE COURAGE TO COME INTO A NEW COUNTRY; HOW FATE PLAYED AGAINST HIM, AND A NEIGHBOR LOOKED LONGINGLY AT HIS RANCH

Looking back now, after so many months of struggle and foreboding, he wondered how he had ever had the high courage to come to this strange country. Had he been a few years older he would not have started forth - he was sure of that now. But the flame of youth was in him, the sure sense that he could conquer where others had miserably failed; and, like all virile young Americans, he had love of adventure, and zest for the unknown was in his blood. The glamour of Arizona lured him; the color of these great hills and mountains he had come to love captivated him from the first. It was as if a siren beckoned, and he had to follow.

For days he had been worried almost to the breaking point. Things had not shaped themselves as he had planned. Event piled upon event, and now disaster - definite disaster - threatened to descend upon him.

All morning, despite the intense heat, he had been about the ranch, appraising this and that, mentally; pottering in the shed; looking at his horses - the few that were left! - smiling at the thought of his wheezing Ford, wondering just when he would clear out altogether.

Not that young Gilbert Jones was a pessimist. And yet he wasn't one of those damnable Pollyanna optimists he so abominated - the kind who went about saying continually that God was in His heaven and all was right with the world. No, indeed! He was just a normal, regular fellow, ready to face a difficult situation when it came about as the natural result of a series of events. He saw the impending catastrophe as the logical finale of many happenings - for some of which he was not in any way responsible.

Who could have foreseen the Great War, for instance? Surely *that* was not his fault! A pitiful archduke was murdered in a European city. He remembered reading about it, and then instantly dismissing it from his mind as of no consequence. He never connected himself with so remote an event. Yet a few years later he, with many others, was fighting in France - a lieutenant in the United States Army - just because a shot had been fired at a man he had never heard of!

A strange world, he pondered, as he looked out over the blue hills, heavy with heat, and meandering away to God knows where.

Then, surely it was no fault of his if the Government under which he lived made no strenuous effort to stop the Mexican massacres of American citizens all along the border. One firm word, one splendid gesture, and daring raids would have ceased; and there would have been no menace of bandits hereabouts. It would have been a country fit to live in. There would have developed a feeling of permanence and peace, and a young chap could have made his plans for the future with some sense of security and high optimism. Surely they were entitled to protection - these brave boys and stalwart sons of America who fearlessly took up claims, staked all, and strove to make homes in this thrilling section along the borderland. They were not mere adventurers; they were pioneers. They were of the best stuff that America contained - clean-cut, clear-eyed, with level heads and high hearts. Yet their own Government did not think enough of them to offer them the sure protection they were entitled to.

Gilbert looked back on that distant day when he had gone up to Bisbee and purchased four head of cattle, and brought them himself to this ranch he had purchased, happy as only a fool is happy. Within a week they had mysteriously disappeared.

Rumors of Mexican thieves and assassins had come to him, as they had come to all the young land-owners along the line. He recalled how, after one raid, in which a good citizen had been foully murdered in his bed, he had called a meeting of the ranchers in their section, and with one voice they agreed to send a protest to Washington.

They did so. Nothing happened. An aching silence followed. They wrote again; and then one day a pale acknowledgment of their communication came in one of those long and important-looking unstamped envelopes. It seemed very official, very impressive. But mere looks never helped any cause. They were not naive enough to expect the Secretary of State to come down in person and see to the mending of things. But a platoon of soldiers - a handful of troops - would have worked wonders. Jones always contended that not a shot would have to be fired; no more deaths on either side would be necessary. The mere presence of a few men in uniform would have the desired effect. The bandits, now prowling about, would slink over the invisible border to their own territory, and never be heard of again. Of that he felt confident.

But no! Watchful waiting was the watchword - or the catchword. And the eternal and infernal raids went on.

It was while they were having their community meeting that he had come to know Jasper Hardy and his young daughter Angela, who occupied the next ranch, about a mile and a half south of his. Before that he had been too busy to bother about neighbors. "Red" Giddings, his foreman, had spoken once or twice about "some nice folks down the line," but he hadn't heard much of what he said. There were always a hundred and one odd jobs to be done around the place - something was forever needing attention; and when Uncle Henry wasn't grumbling about something, he was forcing his nephew to play checkers or cribbage or cards with him. And, working so hard all day, he was glad to turn in early at night. Social life, therefore - unless you could call high words with a crabbed invalid a form of social life - didn't come within Gilbert's ken. It was work, work, work, and the desire to make good every moment for him.

But Hardy proved to be an aggressive fighter when the meeting took place, and spoke in sharp tones of the Government's dilatoriness. He had come to Arizona right after his wife's death in the East, and brought his only daughter and a few servants with him. He seemed to have plenty of money, and he was anxious lest the invading Mexicans should get any of it away from him. His holdings, in the eight years since he had come to the border, amounted to several thousand well-cultivated acres; and he looked like a man who, when he set out to get anything, would get it. He had an inordinate desire to grab up some more territory. Tall and thin, and sharp-featured, as well as sharp-tongued, he resembled a hawk. It was difficult to realize the fact that the pert and lovely little Angela - who lived up to her name only once in a while! - was his own flesh and blood. It was as incongruous as though a rose had grown on a beanstalk.

On their very first meeting, Gilbert had not been pleasantly impressed with Hardy. But he soon saw that the man had a certain rugged strength, and there was no doubt he had suffered from the depredations of Mexico's casual visitors, and was ready to protect not only his own interests but those of any newcomers. He seemed to have the spirit of fair-mindedness; and he believed firmly in the possibilities of this magic land, particularly for young men. "It's God's country," he told Gilbert on more than one occasion. "Get into the soil all you can. Dig - and dig deep."

He said this over and over. It ran like a refrain through every conversation he had with anyone. He preached the gospel of labor. And he did work himself; there was no shadow of doubt as to that. He had struck oil himself, and had made a goodly extra pile. Now, unknown to young Jones, he was casting envious eyes on his ranch; and when the war came and Gilbert went overseas in a burst of fine patriotism, and later came other disasters, he was quick to snatch his opportunity.

Why go to Bisbee, he told Jones, to see who would take up his mortgage? What were neighbors for, if not to come in handy in such unpleasant emergencies? And he laughed.

The long and short of it was that Hardy took an option on Gilbert's property, and held it at this very moment. It was better so, thought Gilbert. Better to be foreclosed by a friendly neighbor, who might hesitate to drive one out at the last moment, than under the thumb of some unknown individual way down the valley.

Four years of it - and he had come to this! Well, he'd take his medicine like a man. He had done his best, and no one could do more.

CHAPTER II

WHEREIN, FAR AWAY, ANOTHER MAN HEARS WHISPERS OF THE WEALTH ALONG THE BORDER, AND COMES DOWN TO SEE ABOUT IT

Up North there was a man with a jaw like a rock, and hard, steel-gray eyes. He had his fingers on the pulse of business, and employed agents everywhere to serve his interests. His office in New York, in the heart of the great financial district, was like a telephone exchange - he the central who controlled the wires, put in and drew out the plugs, and played the fascinating game of connecting himself with any "party" he thought worth while. A shrewd, inveterate gambler, he was without scruples. He lived for one purpose: to make money. For one person: Morgan Pell.

There had been whispers concerning his methods. They were often questionable, to say the least; but, like all men who work quietly beneath the surface of the world of business, Pell covered up his tracks with as much genius as he displayed in consummating a big deal. There should be no loose ends if he was ever charged with corruption. Down in his soul he knew he was a coward. He could not face disgrace, any more than he could face the guns of battle. If his pillow was not always a restful one at night; if he tossed more than he should at his age - he was but thirty-eight - no one knew it. His conscience smote him now and then. In his earlier days he had tricked a widow and caused her to be separated from her last penny. Afterwards, he learned she had committed suicide. He

Charles Hanson Towne

shuddered. In fact, he suffered a little for two long years. Then he forgot about her. Life was life, and though it played unfairly with some, to others it gave beds of roses; and after all we were but puppets of fate, and each must take his chances, and not complain if he did not hold the winning hand. There were only so many to go around. A lottery - that's what it was. And just as people left a card table, a few widows and orphans had to clear out of the big gambling-hall of life. It was as plain as day.

To a man like Pell, a wife was a necessity - but only a secondary consideration. Of course he must marry, keep up an expensive menage, and prove to the world that he was successful even where women were concerned. He must give his wife the proper background, do all the necessary things; furnish the right setting for his jewel. Children? Bah! They were not essential. He had no paternal instinct whatever. Enough that he should support in luxury and affluence the woman he deigned to make his wife, and entertain in his home the people who could and would be of use to him.

Every least act of his life was arranged, specifications written, plans drawn, and blueprints made. One day he decided that he wished a beautiful Italian villa on the north shore of Long Island. He pressed a button, ordered his secretary to get in touch immediately with his architect; and a half-hour later the latter was at his desk ready to talk of the nebulous house. Within twenty-four hours he had arranged everything - not a detail was forgotten.

That is how he did things. He set out to find a wife in the same matter-of-fact manner. He met many women; but Lucia Fennell was the only one who set his pulse beating a little faster. He felt it a shame that he should be so weak. They were at a dinner-party at the country home of a mutual friend.

It was her eyes that held him first. He had never seen quite such eyes - blue, with a curious depth that spoke of many things - the eyes of a girl who, had he been wiser, he would have known had been in love before. This was the type of woman who never loved but once, and then with all her strength beyond her own high dreams of what love should be. But though Pell could appraise men, judge them swiftly and surely, he was a fool where a girl was concerned. He had never spent much time on them. Frankly, they bored him. He liked far better the subtle game of finance. He had no finesse in a world of women, and he would have been the easiest possible prey of an adventuress.

But Lucia was far from that. Of the best family, with old traditions, she moved among the set she wished; but society, so called, did not appeal to her. She preferred people with brains rather than the idle rich; and she had traveled a great deal, and known the world in strange places. She was very young when she met the one man of all men for her. Like all women of great beauty she had known many men who were infatuated with her. Those gifts and attentions which are the rightful dower of every charming girl were hers in abundance; and she received them as a queen might have done from subjects hardly worthy to sit beside her. Then she met - one man.

It was during a trip she had made with her aunt through New England. He was poor. To her, that made no difference. She would have gone with him to the ends of the earth. The flame had touched her heart; she was a victim, like many another; and when her lover, too proud to ask her to share his poverty with her, stayed behind when she went back to New York, and failed to write to her, she almost died of grief. But life had to be faced. One word from her - she, too, was proud, - and there might have been a different story to tell. But with the foolish self-consciousness of lovers, each failed the other in the great moment that would have sealed their destinies.

Lucia determined that this broken affair should not wreck her existence. But she brooded long, in secret, and would go nowhere. Her aunt, with whom she lived, could not rouse her for many months to a sense of the vivid world around her. She would see no one.

Two years later Morgan Pell came into her life, at almost the first dinner she had attended during a long period of time. His impulsiveness, his assurance, his faith in himself and his power to win her, swept her temporarily off her feet. At their second meeting he asked her to become his wife. Why not? She would never love anyone; but she could not go to the altar with him unless she told him the truth. She did not love him. Was he willing to take her, knowing this?

He was. Love meant little to him - though he did not say so. He was just wise enough to keep that secret within himself.

"I'll make you love me," he told her, with all the ardor he could put into his voice. Few women can withstand that age-old phrase.

There followed a time of utter disillusion for her. The great house on the Avenue proved to be but four bleak walls; and when the villa on Long Island was built, she tried to be as enthusiastic as Morgan wanted her to be. He lavished gifts upon her. He brought out gay house-parties for weekends. Lucia did her best to keep her part of a bad bargain. She made herself lovely, and Pell was proud of her physical charms. The jewel was worth the finest settings, and these he supplied, with no thought of the cost. He had someone at the head of his table of whom he was very proud. The world need never know the solemnity of their lives when the curtain was lowered and they were alone together. After all, many marriages were like this. Theirs was by no means an exceptional case; and he experienced a curious secret joy in the fact that he knew other men envied him his wife, and wondered at his power to hold her.

And so the months rolled by, with a trip abroad now and then to relieve the tedium of existence. For a woman to know that she comes to be tolerated only because she is decorative, is a consummating blow. Pell soon reached the point where he told Lucia he had bought her, body and soul. He had determined to win her love. When he saw that he could not, he swiftly forgot the integrity of her part of the bargain, the honesty of her words to him before they were married; and he practised subtle cruelties to tame her and bring her at last to him.

He began to drink too much. Only a certain pride in his business affairs, the desire to keep a level head, a clear brain, kept him from sinking definitely to the gutter. He became irritable with her. Nothing she did pleased him. He found he could not wound her sufficiently when he was sober; so he fortified himself with alcohol, gained courage to speak flat truths, and left her alone for days at a time, thinking such absences were a punishment.

Had he but known it, they were the only bright oases in her monotonous life. She blessed those hours when he mercifully remained away on the pretext of business. What he did gave her little concern.

Once she ventured to talk frankly with him about the wisdom of a legal separation. It was foolish to go on in this way. It was dishonest; it was the only immorality.

He laughed her to scorn. "You're too useful to me, my dear," he sneered. He always added that "my dear" to any statement when he wished to be thoroughly sarcastic.

He was conscious that certain captains of business would not have come so frequently to his home if Lucia had not been there to dispense a supposedly gracious hospitality. Let her go? Lose all this? Not at all! He brutally told her so again and again. And finally she made up her mind, for the sake of peace, that she would merely remain the flower under glass, if that was his desire. Arguments were of no avail. In a sense, she was beaten.

The opera, books, travel, a few good friends - those that Morgan allowed her to keep - these filled her days.

One evening she was particularly surprised when he said to her, casually:

"How would you like a little trip out West? You look peaked. Maybe it would set you up."

"Why - it sounds nice, Morgan," she answered. "Is it business, or -" Her sense of humor made it impossible for her to bring out the word "pleasure."

"Of course it's business," he replied. "Precious little else I get." They were dining alone, at home, and he motioned the butler to refill his glass with champagne.

She wondered at his suggestion. There must be something behind it. But as a matter of fact she was tired of Long Island, and if she could kill a few weeks - maybe a few months - in the West, she would willingly go.

"Sturgis telegraphed me that there was a big possibility of a new vein of oil down on the border," Pell was telling her. "Some important men want to talk things over with me at Bisbee. I want to get started in a day or two. Don't take your maid. It's a rough country, but you'll be all right. Just old clothes. You can ride a lot, so bring your habit. I'll be busy most of the time; but I think you'll like the trip. Never been down that way, have you?"

"No," she said. "And I've always wanted to go."

"Not afraid of bandits?" he laughed, sipping his champagne. "It's right next door to Mexico, you know. Have some swell times down there, they say."

She laughed too. "How exciting," she said. She grew almost jubilant at the prospect of the journey. She knew she would probably be "shown off" to the important men; and that touched her vanity - what little she had left by now.

"They tell me it's God's country, with big chances for everyone. I want to add to our little pile, Lucia," Pell went on. He hoped she would get the significance of the "our."

"You're too good to me, Morgan," she said, and meant it. "But why do we need any more money? We've got everything now."

"Everything?" he said, significantly; and his eyes became two narrow slits as he looked at her.

She toyed with her salad. She hoped he was not going to get into one of his fiendishly unpleasant moods.

"Well," she ventured, "as much as anyone could reasonably want. This house, the garden, friends - "

"Yes," he sneered, "but not much love." The butler had tactfully withdrawn. "Why don't you love me, Lucia?"

"I do - in a way. Oh, let's don't go into all that again, Morgan. We've had it out so many times. What's the use?"

"Is there anyone else?" he asked. "If I thought there was...." He lifted his glass again.

"You know there isn't," she protested.

He appraised her across the table, beautiful in a blue gown which just matched her eyes, her throat adorned with a string of pearls he had given her on the anniversary of their marriage.

"I don't see how a woman as lovely as you can be so cold," he said. "You could do anything with men."

She tried to smile. "But I don't want to. Women - good women - don't like to play with fire. It's only adventuresses who dare to face danger....But let's talk about Arizona. How good it will be to get out of this hothouse of the East, and see real people - real flesh-and-blood men and women."

"Yes. The folks down there know more about life in a day than we do in all our pitiful lives. You've got to live close to nature to understand human nature. Simple, isn't it?"

"Very. We're all so false up here. I get so tired of it, Morgan. Maybe down there we'll come to a better understanding of each other. Maybe...."

"That's what I was hoping. So you'd like to go - really?"

"Yes, indeed. It'll be hot, that's all. But I won't mind that. Anything to get away for awhile."

Two days later they had started. The land was green with early summer, in that rich fullness which makes the heart almost sick with ecstasy. The farther west they went, the wilder the country grew; and when they finally dipped down into Arizona, Lucia looked from the train window, her face alight with joy. Such scenic variety she had never dreamed of. One moment they were looking at the wonderful mesas and superb canyons; the next they seemed to pass through dry gullies and great shallow basins. Then there would come long, weary levels of sand that gleamed in the sun; and far away she would behold tremendous buttes. The valleys they passed through were verdant and lovely. Cattle grazed here in a calm peace. It was as if the rest of the world were shut out, and in this quiet land a special blessing had come down. The peace of it, the stillness of it crowded in upon her. She had been to California, but always she had traveled by a northern route, and had missed the wonder of this part of the world. Before their journey was over, she had begged Morgan to take her to the Grand Canyon; and for two days they remained there, drinking in the glory of perhaps the most beautiful spot on the western continent. She could not get enough of it - those colors that sank into her heart and consciousness and made her think she was in paradise. To see the sun rise here - she almost wept that morning when the lord of heaven came over the mountains that towered like huge sentinels, impervious to wind and gale and rain.

"I can't stand such beauty, Morgan," she said at last. "It takes something out of me. We'll have to go on."

She saw the giant cactus in full bloom, a miracle of orange, pink, and crimson; and as they sped south the mountainsides were aflame with juniper and manzanita.

At last they reached the little town of Bisbee, where Morgan was to have a conference with several engineers. Sturgis met them - a fair-haired fellow with a captivating smile. He liked this country, and told Pell he wished he could always be kept here. There was no doubt about the new vein of oil, and new ranches were being opened up rapidly. Only a few miles away was one that promised well; and the young chap on it was in money difficulties. A good chance to step in. There had been rumors that a neighbor had taken up his mortgage; but maybe this was not so. Perhaps they weren't too late. He had telephoned over, and the youngster had agreed that Pell and his wife could come and stay with him and his invalid uncle for awhile. Of course he knew nothing of their intentions. That would never do. They would just lie low. In fact, he, Sturgis, need not accompany them, except to the hotel. The ranch-owner's foreman would fetch them out in a Ford. Not a bad trip at all - only a few miles. It would be better to stop down there. They could comb the country, get acquainted, see how things were, and keep a vigilant eye on everything.

Sturgis had arranged things nicely. "Red" Giddings came over, as planned, and Lucia liked his pleasant face at once. He was full of enthusiasm for the country, loved the outdoor life. "Mr. Jones has had hard luck, though," he said, as they whirled along the road on an afternoon of unbelievable heat.

"Jones!" Lucia said.

"Yes - Gilbert Jones," Giddings replied. "Ever hear of him?"

For an instant Lucia could hardly see the valley that spread around them. But it couldn't be possible! It was a common name; there could easily be two Gilberts - fifty, for that matter. Was this the reason Morgan had asked her to come? Had he discovered the man with whom she had once been in love, and was this to be one of his subtle punishments? He had told her not to bring her maid, and he had been mysterious, she remembered now, as to their exact destination. But Sturgis had made it clear, on the contrary, that he had accidentally learned of Jones's ranch. Maybe that was part of the trick. But what good would come of such a scheme? She and Jones had loved - and parted. Moreover, perhaps she was giving herself needless cause for worry. This might not be the Gilbert Jones of her dreams. And what if Morgan did know? There was nothing to conceal.

"How - long has he been here?" Lucia wanted to know.

"Oh, before the war we agreed to try our fortune together down here," "Red" told her; and the little machine went whirring along. "That's the Hardy ranch," he said, pointing to the left. "Nice folks." His eyes seemed to cling to the low house, and Lucia did not realize it at the time, but he slowed up the car. Presently a young girl came out on the stone terrace and waved to him. She was like a prairie flower. "Red" Giddings became another man in the twinkling of an eye. A flush mounted to his cheeks, and a smile as broad as a fat man's belt all but encircled his countenance. He took one hand from the wheel and waved until they were out of sight down a curve in the road.

"Friend of yours?" said Morgan Pell, smiling.

"You bet! No finer little girl in this territory!" Giddings replied promptly.

They were now in sight of the Jones ranch. "There she is!" "Red" cried. "Pretty, eh?"

The low adobe house, with its gleaming roof, looked like a jewel set in the valley. Far away, seemingly to the very rim of the world, the flat lands stretched; and then beyond, in a golden haze, the stern mountains loomed, almost kissing the sky. The range dwindled away in an endless line, and one could never say where the boundary of Arizona stopped and the unseen border of Mexico began. The two countries simply merged in the mist. It was as if a battalion of petrified soldiers kept eternal guard in the sun, half the line loping over into another camp, but never caring at all. In the still heat of the afternoon, sagebrush lifted its bright face to the heavens; and now and then a lonely bird swooped above the rich ranches and desolate valleys, making a black dot against the sky. A soft wind was blowing now, bringing mercy from the west, and silence brooded like an angel, stretching out its wings as though to shelter a troubled world.

A young man with black hair and tanned skin came out in the yard, hatless. A gray flannel shirt and a flowing tie, high leggings that laced through many brass clips, completed his picturesque costume.

One look - and she knew it was Gilbert - *her* Gilbert. He recognized her at the same instant, and a curious light came into his dark eyes. She had been thinking, all the way down the road, how she should greet him if indeed he turned out to be that one man in the world. Calmly, yes. She was sure now that Morgan knew and suspected nothing. It was simply a coincidence that they should be coming to the adobe of this old love of hers. The long arm of fate had reached out and snatched her into this ring. She knew that Gilbert could meet the situation as seemingly unconcerned as she. There was nothing at all to fear.

He was their host, and he greeted them as only a good host knows how. Fortunately, Morgan wanted to go directly to his room. He was cross and tired, he said, and he desired to freshen up.

She got out of the car, and "Red" rattled down to the home-made garage a few rods away.

They were alone; and they stood there in the path for a moment, looking into each other's eyes.

"He is my husband," Lucia then found herself saying. "I am now Mrs. Pell."

"What are we going to do?" Gilbert asked. He had the face of a dreamer, she thought. The steel-gray eyes were full of fire and longing. What had these few years done to him?

"We are going to do nothing at all. What *is* there to do? We shall not be here many days. If you'd rather we went back to Bisbee...."

"Oh, no! That would only make an issue of nothing. He doesn't know anything? You're sure? Oh, Lucia!" He seemed suddenly overcome at their amazing meeting.

She saw that she would have to be the mistress of the situation. "Don't - don't, Gilbert," she begged. "I am just a guest of yours."

"I know - I know," he said, and there was a shade of anguish in his voice. "Forgive me. There shall be absolutely nothing said. Not even a gesture. I promise you that. It is as though we had never known each other."

"Surely we can play a part. It isn't as if we were children," she said, and smiled.

He looked at her - indeed, his eyes had never left her face. Never had she seemed so wonderful to him.

"I'm in bad," he told her. "Got to give the old place up. But what's that to you?" There was a sound behind them. "Here comes Uncle Henry!"

A wheel chair came out of the doorway. In it sat an old man of about sixty. But he did not look much like an invalid. His cheeks were rosy, and his abundant white hair was brushed back from a forehead of fine moulding. His eyes were penetrating - as young as Gilbert's, almost. Ten years before he had become paralyzed in his legs, and now he wheeled himself about, not at all uncomfortable.

"Uncle Henry, this is Mrs. Pell. Come out and meet her," his nephew said.

Lucia felt that she should go to the invalid; but he beat her to it. Quick as a billiard-ball he had reached her side, turning the wheels of his chair with great rapidity.

"Pleased to meet you," he said, and put out a white hand. "How long you goin' to stay?"

"What a question," Gilbert laughed. "As long as she and her husband wish, of course."

"Well, by cricketty ginger!" Henry Smith exclaimed. "Hope you'll give 'em enough to eat!" And before anyone could say another word, he had turned and scooted back into the house.

"Don't mind Uncle Henry," Gilbert said to Lucia. "He's got a heart of gold, but he can be cranky and eccentric sometimes. Maybe he's got one of his moods to-day. I never know. Tomorrow he'll be all right - perhaps. I hope so, anyhow.... But come inside. You must be tired after your trip. Your rooms are upstairs."

He led her into the prettiest low-beamed room she thought she had ever seen. Indian pottery was all about, low settles, a fireplace that conjured up a cozy picture of lonely winter evenings, and an entrancing staircase without a balustrade that led to a dark blue door. On the walls were some beautiful Navajo blankets, and a tiny alcove off to the right seemed to lead to another part of the long low house. The windows were brightly curtained, and all the furniture had a look of endurance and permanence - a manly room, she thought. Yet

Charles Hanson Towne

how ironical this appearance of firmness and stability was, in view of the reason of their visit! He had said he must give the place up. What a wrench it would be for him!

Women seldom like to see a bachelor - particularly a young bachelor - living in such solid comfort. As Lucia went up the stairs, she saw little touches she could give to the place. But she had to confess that the improvements she could suggest were not at all important. If two men could get along so well without feminine society, perhaps one of them didn't miss her much, after all!

CHAPTER III

WHEREIN UNCLE HENRY SPEAKS HIS MIND
- AS USUAL

It was high noon, two days later. Gilbert again had been about the ranch looking things over. He had his dreamy moments, but he was far too practical to let the poet in him rule his life. One sensed, by the most cursory glance, that here was a type of virile young American who could not only dream, but make his dreams come true. No idler he! And he had no use for idlers. He had dared to come to this far country, establish himself on a ranch, and seek to win out in the face of overwhelming odds.

How many other young men had staked all on a single game - and lost. That was one of the finest qualities of the Americans who migrated to this vast section of the country. They were always good losers, as well as modest winners. The land was rich in possibilities, as Sturgis had told Pell; and though the hot season lasted interminably and caused one's spirits, as well as one's hopes, to droop, there were enchanting spring days and bright, colorful, dwindling autumns when the air was keen and clear, and life was a song with youth for its eternal theme.

Men with families bore the hardest burdens in their early struggle for success. Gilbert, being single, had less to worry about than many another; but his Uncle Henry was a handicap. For Uncle Henry used his invalid's chair much as a king might use his throne - a vantage place from which to hurl

Charles Hanson Towne

his tyrannous speeches. And there was no come-back. Uncle Henry had reigned too long to be fearful of any retort from any mere subject who walked about on two firm legs. For ten years he had held court, moving his little throne about with sudden jerks. When things did not go entirely his way, he could always withdraw - expertly, swiftly, cleverly. Doorsills were nothing to him. He skimmed them dexterously, as a regiment might storm a hill. Fortunately, he suffered no pain, though sometimes, in a frenzy, he affected a twinge in his body, and caused a helpless look to sweep over his countenance. As a rule, this trick worked beautifully; for who could be cruel to an invalid in pain? Being a bachelor, and having no relative closer than Gilbert, the latter took him under his roof. He really liked the old boy, despite his querulousness.

To-day, Uncle Henry was in one of his temperamental moods. Gilbert, sitting calmly at the little table, writing, in the low main room of the adobe, could hear the chair whirling about, each wheel vocal, and revealing the state of mind of the occupant.

"Gosh! ain't it hot!" finally came from Uncle Henry, his voice a drawl.

Gilbert said nothing. There was nothing to say. Of course it was hot; and he knew Uncle Henry could be depended upon to continue any conversation once begun. Sure enough, it wasn't the weather at all that he was deeply interested in, but the forthcoming midday meal. "Say, ain't we never goin' to eat? I'm as hungry as a bear."

"Dinner ought to be ready now," Gilbert answered patiently, never looking up from his paper.

Uncle Henry was not satisfied. "Then why ain't it," he rasped, giving his chair a twist, "I ain't had nothin' but a rotten cup of coffee since five o'clock this mornin'."

His nephew rose, and went over to the mantel-piece. How

often he had heard just that remark! He didn't bother to reply to it. Instead, he merely silenced his uncle with a gesture. Uncle Henry didn't like being silenced. He looked around, as peevish as a spoiled child, and picked at the cloth that rested on his knees. Then he switched his chair within reach of the table, and snatched up a newspaper, much as a boy might grab the brass ring at a merry-go-round. He would read, if he couldn't make his nephew talk; and he buried himself in the printed page. Gilbert, having lighted his pipe, went back to his writing. "Well, what do you know about that!" exclaimed Uncle Henry, his face aglow.

"About what, Uncle?"

"Why, Ezry Pringle's dead."

"Who's Ezry Pringle?" Gilbert asked, feigning an interest he did not feel.

"A friend o' mine. Only seventy years old, too. He was right in the prime of life."

Gilbert smiled. "What's that paper you're reading?"

"The *Bangor Daily Commercial*, printed at Bangor, Maine. An' that's the only decent town in the whole gol darn world. Wisht I was there now!" He glanced at the alcove that led to another room, as if conscious that Morgan Pell might have heard him. He wanted to say something more to Gilbert, but something told him he had better keep silent. Instead, he read an item from the paper aloud to him. "Listen to this, Gilbert," he said: "'The Elite Fish Market has just received five barrels of soft clams from Eastport. Get there early, feller citizens! They won't last long.' Think o' that, Gilbert? Clams!" He smacked his lips, and even forgot how warm it was. "Clams! An' I ain't even seen one in five long years! Not even a clam!" He turned his chair suddenly, and looked out of the open door, where the country meandered away. "This is a hell of a hole! Why did we ever come down here?" he whined. He swung about again, and faced his nephew. "Say, Gil, do they have clams in France?"

"No; only mussels. Good ones, too."

Uncle Henry looked amazed. "They eat mussels?" he cried.

Gilbert looked up, smiled, and nodded.

"An' I hear they eat frogs, an' hosses, an' cheese with worms in it, too. Say," the old man wanted to know, "what don't they eat over there?...An' speakin' of eatin', ain't we never goin' to have no dinner?"

"I think it'll be ready soon, Uncle. Do be patient. I want to write."

Uncle Henry settled back in his chair, and for a brief interval became absorbed in his newspaper. But not for long could he remain silent. "Where's that Mr. Pell?" he asked.

"Inside, I think, lying down," Gilbert replied, nodding toward the alcove, his pen rushing across the page.

Uncle Henry made a grimace. "He makes me sick, that feller."

"Oh, cut that out, Uncle," Gilbert implored; but there was a little note of irritation in his voice. "That's no way to talk of a guest under our roof."

"I won't neither cut nothin' out! An' you make me sick too, you gol darn fool!"

"For the love of Mike, quit your babbling! Sssh!"

"Don't you shush me, gol darn it!" cried Uncle Henry, crumpling the newspaper in his hand and throwing it on the floor. The heat was affecting him. "I've kep' still long enough, an' -"

"Oh, have you?" Gilbert smiled.

"- an' I'm goin' to find out what's what!" Uncle Henry went on, as though he had not been interrupted.

"You act as though I were to blame for what's happened," his nephew said. He saw it would do no good to lose his temper.

"Well, ain't you? Why did you want to go to war in the first place? Why, why?" He pounded the arm of his chair. "That's what started it."

"Well, somebody had to go," Gilbert answered, smiling. "If some of us hadn't taken things in our hands, I don't know what would have become of Democracy!"

Uncle Henry pondered a moment. "Mebbe so. But you didn't have to go." Gilbert had risen to get a match, and his uncle's eye followed him to the mantel-piece. He spoke to the back of his head. "You could have claimed exemption if you'd wanted to, an' you know it."

"Exemption?" Gilbert repeated the word, a little angry at its utterance. This wasn't like Uncle Henry who, with all his peculiarities, had always been a patriot.

"Absolutely! You were the sole support of an invalid uncle." He waited for the truth of this remark to sink in; but Gilbert said nothing. "And on top of that," Uncle Henry went on, rapidly, when his nephew did not speak, "you were engaged in an essential industry - if you can call these rotten steaks you feed us on essential. The bones is softer than the meat." He gave a curious little laugh, thin and high.

Gilbert went back to the table, leaned over, and put one hand affectionately on the old man's shoulder. "Now, Uncle," he said, kindly, "what's the use of going over all this again? You know how I dislike it." He sat down and began to write again. But Uncle Henry had not finished - he had just started.

"What's the *use*?" he wheezed. "There's lots of use. Here you go an' persuade me to sell the old home and buy this rotten ranch 'way down here in this God-forsaken country. An' just when I, like a darned old fool, take an' do it, along comes the war an' you enlist and leave me here with nothin' but a lot of rotten cows!"

"But I left the foreman and the cook," Gilbert reminded him.

A look of scorn came over Uncle Henry's face, "Yes, 'Red' Giddings - playin' the harmonicky until I go almost crazy! An' a Mexican cook that can't cook nothin' but firecrackers! An' not even them when you want 'em!" He waited for this crowning touch to sink in. Infuriated by Gilbert's indifference, he swung around again in his chair. "Say, ain't we *never* goin' to have no dinner? I'm hungry!"

"I'm sorry," was all Gilbert said.

Uncle Henry almost resorted to tears - they were in his voice, at any rate. "First you rob me an' then you starve me!" he all but screamed. "An' the best you got to say is you're sorry!"

Jones never looked up, as he continued to write. "I did the best I could, Uncle. You know that, of course."

A remark like that always exasperates the hearer. "If that's yer best, I'd hate to see what yer worst is like," the other flamed. "An' now we're broke, an' they're goin' to foreclose to-day!" he added. "By golly, mebbe they've foreclosed already!"

"No, not till eight o'clock," Gilbert's passionless manner was maddening.

"Eight o'clock to-night?" his uncle cried, and leaned so far out of his chair that he was in danger of falling to the floor.

"Yes," Gilbert said, calmly.

"You're crazy! Don't you know yet that courts don't stay open at night?" He swung about in his frenzy and disgust.

"This court does. Somebody told the judge where he could get a bottle of liquor for eighteen dollars," Gilbert added, and smiled.

"So if we don't get ten thousand dollars there by eight o'clock to-night, we're set out on the bricks without no more home than a prairie dog - not as much!" almost screamed Uncle Henry. "An' yet you say why talk about it?"

"But it isn't getting us anywhere - just to sit around and complain," his nephew tried to pacify him, rising, and starting toward him again; but Uncle Henry didn't want to be so near him, knowing what he was going to say next. Therefore he switched adroitly to the door, and let out, "No, it ain't gettin' us anywhere; but it would if you'd marry Angela Hardy, like I want you to!" He was a little frightened now that he had uttered the words, and he looked anxiously at Gilbert to see their effect. The latter remained as calm as ever. "But I don't love her," was all he said.

Uncle Henry was exasperated now. "What's that got to do with it?" he yelled. "Her father's rich, an' not even he, mean as he is, would foreclose on his own son-in-law. Mebbe he'd even lend you somethin' besides," he added, slyly. He had great faith in these neighbors down the valley.

"I can't do it," Gilbert stated, as if he were discussing going to the nearest town.

"Won't, you mean."

"No. I mean can't - just what I said. It wouldn't be fair to her. I can't pretend to love her when I don't."

"You don't have to," his uncle urged. "She's so crazy about you, she'd marry you anyway." Triumphant knowledge was in his tone.

"What makes you think so?" Gilbert asked, coming close to the old man.

"She told me she would." He got it out bravely.

Young Jones was nearly bowled over. "She told you!" he repeated; and as he said it, passion for the first time came into his voice. There was the sound of hoof beats down the road. But neither of them paid any attention.

"Absolutely," the old man affirmed.

"Absolutely?"

"Absogoshdarnlutely!" Uncle Henry relieved the tension by saying.

Gilbert came over and peered into his uncle's face. "You don't mean you spoke to her about it?" he said.

"Why not?" rather impudently. "Somebody had to do it." And he chuckled. "I know what would become of Hypocricy if a few of you youngsters would be as brave as us old boys!"

"Good Lord!" was all young Jones could say, and he put his hand to his head.

"John Alden spoke for Miles Standish, an' they wasn't even related," Uncle Henry tried to placate the other.

The horse on the road, unknown to the men, had reached the adobe. Lucia Pell, radiant as a prairie flower, appeared at the door. She wore a riding-habit that fit her to perfection, and her hair, tumbled a bit by the soft breeze, fell around her face in a cascade of golden loveliness. Her eyes sparkled. She was the picture of glorious health and youth - a woman born for love and loving. She brought fragrance into the room.

"Hello, Gil!" she said, beating her riding-crop on her boot, and smiling that entrancing smile of hers. She was glad to see her handsome host again after her brisk ride.

"Good morning, Lucia," Gilbert said, hardly daring to look at her.

Uncle Henry didn't mean to be overlooked. "Good afternoon, Mrs. Pell," he said, meaningly.

"Why, it *is* afternoon, isn't it?" she laughed.

"It's darn near night," Uncle Henry rasped.

"And I'm simply famished. Who wouldn't be, after such a glorious ride!" Lucia said.

"The cook's getting dinner now. Have a good canter, you say?" young Jones inquired.

"I missed you," Lucia answered, unashamed.

Uncle Henry looked disgusted.

"I'm sorry, I had a lot of things to attend to. I'm glad you're back, for I was beginning to be worried about you, Lucia. Bandits! They're around again."

Lucia didn't take him seriously. She hardly remembered that they were so close to the border of Mexico. "Bandits?" she scoffed. "Oh, but they just steal cows and things, don't they?"

"Worse than that." Gilbert was serious, and gave her an appraising glance. "Human life means little in Mexico. They even kill their prisoners in cold blood."

But still Lucia was not alarmed. "If that's true," she smiled, "I won't go without you, if you wish it that way." She looked knowingly at him.

"It isn't what I wish," Jones answered. "Nothing is what I wish."

"Well," Uncle Henry put in, "you're going to get your wish all right." As he spoke, Morgan Pell came through the alcove from his room, and the old invalid steered his chair so that he faced him. Pell looked anything but engaging to-day. There was something about him that repelled - people could never say what it was; but one sensed a latent cruelty in the man. His eyes were shifty, and there were little lines about his mouth that spoke of his days of dissipation. It was hard to associate him with the flower-like Lucia. Here were a man and woman never meant for each other - that was evident immediately; yet he had that old power that seemed to hypnotize her. And she was not the only woman who had fallen beneath his spell. But now, apparently, he did not see her.

"Good afternoon, Mr. Pell," said old Smith to the newcomer.

"How are you?" the latter answered, with no show of interest.

"Have a good nap?" Gilbert inquired; but he really didn't care at all. Pell, however, took his question seriously.

"Couldn't sleep a wink," he said. "This cursed heat, you know. Glad I don't have to live in this part of the world all the time."

Uncle Henry leaned forward in his chair, and his eyes followed Pell expectantly as the latter moved across the low room, a small satchel in his hands. "You ain't leaving, are you?" he asked.

"No," was the laconic reply.

"I was afraid you wasn't," ventured Uncle Henry; and there was an awkward pause. Then, "It's pretty hot," the invalid remarked, delighted that no one had called him to account for his obvious insult. He knew he had all the advantage of a weak woman. His little throne was immune from attack.

"It's always pretty hot till night - then it's pretty cold," Pell said.

"What've you got that bag for?" Uncle Henry pursued. No one was ever more frankly curious than Uncle Henry.

"Company, my dear sir," Pell quickly retorted, not a little annoyed at the question; and he glared at the old man. He had had two days of him, and was getting used to him. Lucia, who had remained silent by the door, saw the cloud on her husband's face, and gave a little, startled "Oh!" It was hardly more than a whisper, but Pell was swift to catch it. He turned on her, and took in her radiant figure.

"So there you are!" he half sneered. "Been riding?"

"Yes; just a little canter."

"Alone?" Pell followed up.

"Yes; why?"

"Oh, nothing - nothing at all." There was a nasal tone in his voice always - a twang that grated on sensitive ears. He turned on Gilbert. "How about dinner?" he asked, almost as though the young fellow were a hotel clerk.

"It isn't ready yet," Jones answered. He disliked the other's tone. After all, he was a guest in his, Gilbert's, house. He hoped their wretched business would soon be settled, and Pell return to New York. He had had his fill of him.

Pell, seemingly oblivious of the bad impression he had made, started toward the door. He had not put the bag down. "Well, call me when dinner *is* ready, will you? I won't be far away."

"Where are you going?" Lucia ventured.

"Out," was Pell's curt reply; and he almost knocked Uncle

Henry's chair aside as he hurried into the yard.

There was an awkward silence at his departure. Everyone felt a little ashamed for him; but Gilbert was determined that Lucia should not read his thoughts. So he said, nonchalantly, "Well, Lucia, how did the pony behave?" just as though Pell had never been in the room.

"Splendidly!" the young wife replied, glad that the atmosphere was cleared once more. "Oh, Gil, it's wonderful here - nothing but sky and the golden desert! What a miracle place!"

"You like it here?" Jones asked, knowing that she did. She had told him so every hour of her visit.

Lucia gave him a rapt look. "Like it, Gil? Um! I love it!" She clasped her hands to her breast; and Jones thought she had never looked lovelier, more desirable. How pink her cheeks were! Yet underneath her beauty there was a wistful sadness. Anyone could see that she was not happy.

"You really love it?" Uncle Henry asked, as though he could not believe he had heard what she said.

Lucia had forgotten his presence for a moment. Now she turned to him and smiled. "Of course. Don't you?"

"It makes me sick!" was the unexpected reply.

Lucia was horrified; and she looked from Smith to Gilbert in utter confusion. "Why, it's beautiful!" she exclaimed.

"Beautiful!" Uncle Henry went on, repeating the word in derision. "What's beautiful about it? That's what I'd like to know."

"The desert," Lucia answered.

"A lot of gol darn sand!" the invalid whined.

"The sky, then!" Lucia affirmed.

But Uncle Henry merely repeated "The sky!" in whole-hearted disgust.

Lucia refused to be downed. "But think of the glorious colors - blue and gold and purple!"

"And no grass nor nothin'," the invalid retorted. "Not even a place to go fishin'. And you call it beau - Say, was you ever in Bangor?"

Gilbert roared with laughter; but Lucia took the old boy seriously. "Bangor?" she repeated, wonderingly.

"Yes. Bangor, Maine. Now there's a place as is beau - Take the town hall, for instance. And the Soldiers' Monument. And the cemetery. They got the swellest cemetery in Bangor you ever -." Gilbert was almost doubling up with laughter; but Uncle Henry went right on: "As for this gol darn place, I wish it was in - An' it wouldn't have fur to go, neither!" he added, emphatically, smiling at his own humor. "I wisht I was back in Maine! There's where I was always so happy!"

By this time Lucia was smiling too. She went over and shook her finger gently in the invalid's face. "You're cross just because you're hungry!"

"I ain't neither!" Smith replied, like a little boy.

"Yes, you are!" Lucia kept on.

"I ain't!"

"Uh, uh!" she teased him, as though she were playing with a baby.

Smith grew peevish. "Gol darn it, I tell you I ain't!" And he gave his chair a rapid twirl.

"Boo!" came from Lucia softly. She laughed, and ran up the tiny stone stairs that led to her room.

"Boo, yourself!" called out Uncle Henry, determined to have the last word, as Lucia disappeared. Then he turned querulously on his nephew, as soon as he was certain she was out of hearing. "Why did you ever invite 'em to stay here in the first place?" he wanted to know. The sound of "Red's" harmonica was heard outside.

"Because there was no decent hotel anywhere near. I couldn't do less than offer them what little hospitality I had, could I, when Sturgis suggested it?"

But his uncle didn't agree with him at all. "You could have done a whole lot less," he decided. "You could have invited 'em to keep on going. Comin' here at a time like this, and not only eatin' us out of house and home, but drinkin' up the last bottle of liquor in the world!" This seemed to him the culminating tragedy. When his nephew said nothing at all, he asked, petulantly, "Well, what are you going to do? That's what I want to know."

"What can I do?"

"Do you mean to say you're going to set here and get throwed out into the street and not even try to do something?"

Gilbert merely shrugged his shoulders.

"Well, of all the -" his Uncle Henry went on. "It's a darn good thing for you that I'm an invalid! That's all I got to say!" He wheeled about, and aimed at the door that led to the open air. At that instant "Red" Giddings, the husky young foreman, appeared directly in his path, his shock of fiery hair like an aureole about his head. "Git out o' my way!" Uncle Henry yelled. "Gol darn the gol darn luck, anyhow!"

And through years of practice he shot into the yard as straight as an arrow.

Charles Hanson Towne

CHAPTER IV

WHEREIN "RED" REVEALS HIS HEART,
AND MRS. QUINN GIVES HIM GOOD COFFEE
AND GOOD ADVICE

"Red" Giddings had been on the ranch with Gilbert since the very beginning. He came from the North with the young man, willing to stake all on this one venture. Like young Jones, he was not afraid. He was an efficient, well-set-up young fellow, with three consuming passions: Arizona, his harmonica, and Angela Hardy. The first saw a lot of "Red"; the second touched his lips frequently; but as for Angela - well, perhaps the poor boy kissed his harmonica so often in order to forget her lips. But if his own music charmed "Red," it failed to have that effect upon others - particularly Uncle Henry, who went into a rage whenever he heard the detested instrument. "Red's" music had no charms to soothe the savage breast of Henry Smith.

But another did like it. Angela once told "Red" in the moonlight - and her father had never forgiven her for her foolishness - that his harmonica never wearied her. That was enough for "Red." Once every day he managed to find some excuse to get over to the Hardy ranch; and always his beloved instrument went along with him in his pocket, and he would approach his lady love's castle like the troubadours of old, his foot tapping on the path while his harmonica, in the place of a lute, made soft sounds. Instantly Angela would poke her pretty head from the window, and pretend that she was a princess in distress, and he her knight who had come to release her from her prison.

Moreover, the Hardys had a wonderful cook - a woman they had brought down from Phoenix. Instead of the firecracker stuff that Uncle Henry so bitterly complained of, she, being an Irish woman, could concoct a stew that would make one's hair curl; and her pastry was succulent and sweet, and literally melted in the mouth. Her coffee - ah! who could make better coffee? And as the meals at the Jones ranch were served sporadically, and "Red" was as healthy as a peasant and had never known the time when he couldn't tuck away some dainty from the kitchen he ingratiated himself with Mrs. Quinn, quite won her heart, too, with his music, and was even known to desert his work for the boon of a bit of pie.

When she was suffering from the heat of the stove, and was ready to throw up her job and return to the bright lights of Phoenix, "Red" invariably came around to the door with music on his lips, his shock of hair blown by the soft wind, looking so boyish that she had to succumb to him, boil another pot of coffee, and lay a place for him at the corner of the table.

"Be off wid yez!" she always began by saying. But the insinuating harmonica was his only reply; and she ended by begging him to come in and play for her while she messed with the pots and pans, and maybe found some batter for a plate of griddle cakes.

On this particular morning, work being useless since things were going so badly for Jones, "Red" slipped up the road and reached the kitchen door just as Mrs. Quinn was washing up.

"Oh, so there ye be, me boy!" was her motherly greeting. "Come in, an' maybe - who knows? - I'll find a cup o' coffee fer ye, though I'm not thinkin' ye deserve it."

"Red" loved the odors from this fragrant kitchen. The stove always gleamed, and when Mrs. Quinn was in good humor she was like a great light moving here and there, dispensing warmth also. She was a monstrous woman; but like many large people, she got about easily and swiftly. Her capable hands were forever fluttering in the flour-barrel or over the dough-board, and her ruddy cheeks and honest gray eyes spoke of health and good nature. She adored Angela; and she really liked "Red" tremendously, and hoped in the end he would win the difficult and fickle girl. But, like Angela, she had moment when she could have shaken him. For "Red" didn't fight hard enough for what he wanted. He was naive to the point of stupidity at times; and women like aggressive men - even men who are capable of flogging them into submission, deny it as they will. "Red" was gentle and mild, though thoroughly manly. Both Angela and Mrs. Quinn would have liked to see him live up to his fiery hair.

He beamed now at the genial cook's greeting, and took out his harmonica, running over the full scale as a suitable answer.

"Here, sit ye down, 'Red,'" Mrs. Quinn ordered. "But first see that yer feet is wiped off. I don't want to see no dirt along me clean floor."

She was busy with a place for him near the window, happy, as most women are, to serve a handsome young chap, and secretly wishing in her heart that she had him for a son.

The coffee was miraculously brought, and soon the griddle-cakes, gloriously brown, and deftly turned by Mrs. Quinn, were in front of him.

"Gee! you make a feller happy, Mrs. Quinn!" said the appreciative "Red," sitting down, and getting busy, "Won't you come to Bisbee with Angela an' me the next time we go to the movies?"

She gave him a half-scornful look. "An' what would yez want with an old woman like meself taggin' along with yez now?" Mrs. Quinn exclaimed, her arms akimbo. "Ain't ye happy enough with yer Angela, an' no fat funeral like me occupyin' too much room in the Ford? Go along, me lad, an' have a good time with yer colleen! She'd like it better alone with ye, too - be sure o' that!"

"Of course I would!"

They hadn't seen Angela come in. She stood in the doorway like a vision - a morning-glory from which the freshness of the early hours never seemed to depart.

"Oh!" poor "Red" gasped, and leaped to his feet. "Would you, Angela?" He looked at her, drank her beauty in, as though she were the only creature on this earth.

"Certainly!" said Angela, coming over to him. "You're a boob, 'Red,' and if you don't look out, there's a fellow over at Bisbee who - "

"Oh!" the anguished "Red" managed to get out. "*Is* there, Angy?"

There was - of course there was - and there wasn't. Angela knew just how far to go. Her black eyes danced. "Red" sat down again, after she had shoved him back to his late breakfast. Mrs. Quinn, amused, was busy with some more cakes, though "Red" had scarcely had time to begin the first batch. But she knew his capacity, and she felt he would need sustaining food after Angela's last remark.

"You don't always wave to me like you did the other day when I went by," said "Red," his lips in Mrs. Quinn's golden coffee.

"Why should I?" said Angela. "You don't always have such swell-looking folks with you!"

"Oh, so that's why you waved!" disappointment in his tone.

"Maybe." She was teasing him, but he didn't know it. "Who were they?"

"A Mr. and Mrs. Pell, from New York. They're lookin' over property round here....But I don't care, Angy. Even if I had to go to Bisbee four times a day and get some good-lookin' folks to bring down the road, I'd do it if you'd wave to me! Oh, why can't you always be nice to me?"

"If I was always nice to you, you wouldn't know how lucky you are!" she countered. "It's good for you to have your bad days - with me."

"Well, maybe you're right. You're 'most always right; but gosh! a feller does like a little encouragement once in a while. You can be so cruel, Angy!"

"Can I? If you think not waving to you is cruelty, you ought to see some of my other forms of torture."

"Ugh! I hope I never do!" He drank again from the cup.

"Say," Angela said, watching him, "you seem to like that coffee a lot more than you like me! That brunette in the cup is my rival!"

He looked at her in blank amazement. He hadn't much sense of humor. He was as literal-minded as a child. "You certainly are the funniest girl, Angy!" he said, "How could coffee be a girl's rival?"

"Easier than a fellow in Bisbee - maybe. Better look out, 'Red,' or I'll sue Mrs. Quinn for alienation of affections!"

"Oh, you wouldn't do that!" said the kindly, honest "Red."

"What a stupid you are, to be sure!" said Angela, and laughed. "There - eat these hot cakes - though how you can on this beastly warm morning is more than I can see - and then play me some tunes. I'm dying to hear some music. This afternoon Dad says he's going over to your ranch. I don't know what for, do you? I do wish people didn't have to lose their property.

Why are mortgages, anyhow?"

"Blamed if *I* know, Angy! Thanks, Mrs. Quinn."

"Sure, an' you're welcome, me boy." Angela had gone out on the step. The old Irishwoman saw her chance. "For the love o' Mike, 'Red,' woo her, an' woo her hard! There *is* a feller in Bisbee. She's after lovin' ye, but you're too slow - slower'n the molasses I just poured on yer griddle-cakes fer ye!"

"I'll try," said the accommodating "Red." "You're a good friend, Mrs. Quinn. I won't forget you when I own this place!"

"Be off, now! Ye've got some travelin' to do before ye're able to win Angela. Then ye can think of buyin' a ranch."

She literally pushed him from her domain; and he found himself by Angela's side out of doors.

The bright sunlight touched her hair, and they went over to a pergola she had had built, covered with vines. A little fountain tinkled near it, and the heat of the day would not bother them here.

For three delirious hours, "Red" was alone with Angela. One moment she pouted, the next she let him touch her hand.

"You may be going away soon, 'Red.' Will you write to me if you do?"

"Will I?" he cried, "Every day - a postal-card at least. I ain't much at letters....But I'm not so sure I'm goin', Angy. Something tells me that even if your father does hold the mortgage, it won't be foreclosed. Gil Jones has worked too hard...."

"Dad's awfully hard about holding to a bargain," Angela reminded him. "He's all business. He wasn't that way until after Ma died. I do wish he'd be more human. I've talked to him and talked to him, until I'm tired; but he's getting harder all the time. This is the last day, isn't it?"

"Yes. Jones is awful blue. That's one reason I ought to get back. Maybe he needs some cheerin' up. God knows his Uncle Henry don't give him much."

The sun was now high in the heavens. It was almost noon. "Red" said he would walk. No trouble at all; and what did he care how hot it was? He was used to it. But how he did hate to leave his Angela!

He played his harmonica most of the way home, and he was still running his lips along the instrument when he entered the adobe door, just as Uncle Henry wheeled out of it.

CHAPTER V

WHEREIN GILBERT JONES IS WORRIED, AND LUCIA PELL IS ASKED TO DO AN IMPOSSIBLE THING

Poor "Red" couldn't have encountered the invalid at a less propitious moment; for he was almost knocked down by that crabbed gentleman.

"Certainly wheels a mean chair," he said good-naturedly to Gilbert, as he watched Uncle Henry steer himself out to the gate. "Got his cut-out open, too! Pesky to-day, ain't he? That's one reason I came back." He spread his legs apart, and fanned himself with his hat. He ran his fingers through his thick, violent crop of hair. "A mean Arizona day!" he said. "The walk made me hot."

"I should think it would," Jones replied.

"No grub yet?" "Red" ventured. He was hungry even yet. Twenty-two is always hungry.

"No," said his employer.

"Should have been ready two hours ago. What's the matter? Wish we had Mrs. Quinn over here."

"I don't know what's the matter. I haven't thought much about eating." He was engrossed again in his papers.

But "Red" didn't intend to let the matter drop. "You're too easy on that cook," he said. "Now, if you had a Mrs. Quinn -" He had pulled out a worn tobacco-bag, which was discouragingly flat. He had smoked a lot this morning.

Gilbert was swift to notice the empty pouch, and offered him his.

"Thanks; much obliged," "Red" said, filling his pipe. "But darn that cook, anyhow! If he wasn't leavin', I'd fire him! As if you didn't have enough troubles, without havin' to bother about late meals - an' guests in the house."

But a puff or two on his pipe soothed him, "Red's" bark was always worse than his bite. He was the best-natured chap in the world, and he idolized Gilbert Jones. There was a big packing-case in the middle of the room, and he sat on it, tailor-fashion, as happy as a husky, normal young man can be.

He looked longingly at the unset table; but his thoughts were more of Angela Hardy than of the good meal to come.

"'Red,'" said Gilbert after a brief silence, "I was hoping to be able to pay you off to-day."

"Pay me off?" That would have been heaven! He could have taken Angela to the movies at Bisbee.

"Yes."

"Oh, forget it! You don't owe me nothin'!"

"Only a mere trifle of six months' wages," Gilbert laughed.

"Red" had put his head in one hand, and leaned back on the case, at peace with the world. His left foot beat a little tattoo on the side of the box. Now he sat up straight and looked sharply at Jones.

"What's the use of talking about this?" he wanted to know. "You ain't got it, have you?"

Gilbert paused the fraction of a second. "No," he had to admit, "But that doesn't alter the fact that I owe you money." He went over and stood close to his foreman.

"You're wrong," the younger man said. "It was my own proposition that I come here with you and work, an' you know it. Now what you got to say?"

Gilbert put his arm around "Red's" big shoulder, and playfully pushed him off the box. "You're just a big kid, aren't you, 'Red'?"

"I don't know what I am. But I do know I was only too glad to take the gamble with you. An' I'll take another one right now if you've got one to suggest."

Gilbert pushed the case over on its side. It was empty. There were some Navajo blankets on a little stand by the window. These he now fetched over to the case, first placing them carefully on the floor, spread out in all their rainbow beauty. Their bright patterns glorified the room, as if a lamp had been lighted. He said nothing. "Red" wondered what he was doing with these splendid blankets. He had never seen anything like them on the ranch, though there were others on the walls.

"I'd like to remark," "Red" went on, "that if we ever gets into the cow business again, we ought to get us a nice ranch in Washington, D.C. It don't pay American citizens to go too fur away from home, these days."

Gilbert laughed. Then, "Oh!" he ejaculated, as though remembering something.

"What's the matter?" "Red" asked.

"Haven't you heard? Lopez has broken off the reservation again."

"Lopez!" exclaimed "Red," forgetting his pipe, his dinner, and even Angela for the moment. "The devil he has!"

"Uh - uh! Raided the Diamond Dot last night."

"He won't bother us," "Red" smiled, settling back again. "Nothin' to steal here except the mortgage." He paused, as though in deep thought; but Gilbert, had he known it, was thinking even harder. Lopez, the Mexican bandit, was a dim uncertainty; the mortgage was a stern reality.

"You'll want to be drivin' over to the station later?" "Red" went on, coming to the table, and taking off his spurs.

"Yes," Gilbert answered. He had folded all the blankets neatly, rose, and went over to the window-box to get some strong cord.

"In the gallopin' wash-boiler?" "Red" smiled, "*That* still belongs to us - I mean, you." He clinked his spurs on the table.

"Us is right, 'Red.' You said you'd been a partner. You have. Some day I'm going to tell you how grateful I am." In his preoccupation, he forgot to tie up the blankets; and, one hand on "Red's" shoulder, he let the cord fall on the table.

"Aw, that's all right," "Red" said. He didn't like to be thanked, and he avoided even the shadow of sentimentality with Jones. After all, they were two young fellows, playing a big game together, taking big chances; and what was the use of talking about it? "What are you going to tell the Pells?" he suddenly asked, glad to get off the immediate subject.

"Pells?"

"Say, I'm goin' to poke that bird in the beak some day!"

"Red" declared.

Jones smiled. "What's he done to you?"

"Nothin'. He'd better not. It's the way he treats his wife. She's so darn game, too. I wouldn't treat a horse the way he treats her. Well, what are you goin' to tell them?"

Gilbert stood perfectly still. He was in deep thought. Finally he spoke.

"I'm going to tell them I'm going away - important business."

"East?" "Red" asked. He had seated himself at the table, and picked up Gilbert's pen, and began making curious little scrawls with it on a piece of paper, as a business man sometimes does when he is telephoning.

"No. West," answered Jones. "They're going East."

"What are you going to do?" "Red" was amused rather than alarmed.

"Oh, I'll get a job somewhere. Punch cows - or maybe join the rangers. There's always something a fellow can do."

"An' what about your uncle?"

"I'll put him up in Bisbee till I get a chance to ship him back to Bangor. He likes Bangor, you know!" Gilbert smiled.

"He takes it sort o' hard, don't he?"

"Well, you can't blame the old boy. You see, I got him to sell out everything - everything, and invest in this ranch. Maybe it wasn't the right thing to do; but I thought I was certain to succeed. I meant all for the best, 'Red.' You know that." Who could doubt those gray eyes of Gilbert Jones, that open, frank, boyish face?

"Of course I do." He got up, and walked over to the window. "Your uncle don't like jokin' much, does he? I asked him the other day why he didn't get a chauffeur. Gosh! he got mad!" "Red" laughed at the recollection.

"Uncle Henry's in no joking mood just now. You can't blame him much."

"Red" turned and looked at his employer. He didn't know whether he should ask the next question or not; but he took his courage in his hands.

"He - he wants you to - to marry Angela Hardy, don't he?"

Gilbert looked surprised. "Hardy's daughter?"

"Red" nodded.

"How did you know?" Jones asked.

"Because he ain't talked of nothin' else for six months. You wasn't thinkin' of doin' it, was you?" He hung on Gilbert's answer.

"Hardly!" with a smile.

The relief of "Red"!

"I know, I know!" he cried. "But once she gets her mind set on a thing -"

"You mean you think she wants to marry me? Is that it?" Gilbert asked, not taking the matter very seriously. He was busy at the box again, pulling the top farther back.

"Well, I don't know as I'd say that," "Red" offered; "but I think she thinks she wants to." He was sitting on the edge of the table, swinging one leg. "She's prone to fancies, Angela is. Even I gotter admit that!"

"*Even* you?" Gilbert inquired, puzzled.

The question made "Red" a bit nervous. He jumped to the floor, and then sat down in the chair beside the table, pretending to be very much at ease. "Like that traveling man from Saint Looey," he explained. "She thought she cared for him. I tried to tell her different. I had to run him out of town with a gun to prove it. But even then she didn't believe it until that New York surveyor come along."

Gilbert looked up, "And she thought she loved him?"

"Until she met up with that hoss doctor from Albuquerque! An' now there's a new feller in Bisbee!"

Jones was a trifle mystified, "Say, how do you happen to know so much about her affairs, 'Red'?"

How involved he had become! He blushed like a schoolboy; got up, took his pipe out of his mouth and emptied it in the fireplace. "Me?" he said. "Oh, I've knowed her a long time."

Jones was beginning to see the truth, to read the heart of this young rascal. So it was over at the Hardy's that he spent so many hours!

"Oh, so that's it, is it? What's the matter? Does her father object?"

"Oh, no!" "Red" was quick to deny. "I stand all right with him. He's knowed me a long time. It's her."

Gilbert laughed outright; and "Red," humanly embarrassed now that his secret was out, paced the room, his hands behind his back, digging his heel every now and then in the floor. "Aw -" he began.

"Listen, 'Red,'" said Jones, in sympathy with the lad, and hoping to cover up his confusion. "If Hardy comes, keep him out till I'm alone. I don't want any war talk before the Pells."

"I get yer," said "Red," visibly relieved.

"Any stronger cord on the place anywhere?" Gilbert looked around the room. Maybe one of the many Indian jugs contained a string. "Red" and he had a habit of putting any old thing in them.

"There's some down in the hay barn. Want me to get it for you?" "Red" offered.

"No; I'll get it, thanks. You see if you can't prod up the cook a little. I'm hungry now."

And "Red" ran into the kitchen. No sooner had he left the room, than there was a rumble, and Uncle Henry burst in on Gilbert, a smile of triumph on his face.

"I got it!" he all but yelled.

"Got what?" his nephew asked.

"An idea!...Mebbe he'd lend you some."

"Some what? And who?"

"Money, of course! That feller Pell, I mean. He's rich, an' if he knowed that you and his wife was old friends - I betcher he'd lend you some." He paused, breathless, for he had run his sentences into one. Gilbert glared at him, as if he thought he had gone stark mad. But Uncle Henry was not afraid. "You won't ask him?" he inquired.

"Certainly not. What are you raving about, anyhow? Cut out this sort of talk, Uncle. You're getting on my nerves."

The old man simply switched his chair about. He had heard Gilbert in an angry mood before, and he knew that nothing would follow his little burst of wrath. "Oh, you make me tired, you young people," he raged. "I'd ask him if it was me, you can bet I would!"

"*You* would," was all that Gilbert replied. Sarcasm was in his voice.

"First you won't marry Hardy's daughter and now you won't ask him for money," Uncle Henry pursued the subject.

Gilbert was genuinely angry now. "Oh, keep quiet! I'm sick of your plans."

"Yes, but if you ain't goin' to do nothing, I am!"

His nephew wouldn't trust himself to hear another word. He turned on his heel and left the old man.

Uncle Henry was shaking with excitement. He lifted his hand, smote the arm of his chair, and cried out after the vanishing figure of his nephew, "You make me sick, you gol darn fool!" He was almost in tears. "Gol darn the gol darn luck, anyhow!"

At that moment, Lucia Pell came down the little stairway. She had discarded her riding-habit, and now looked equally lovely in a simple frock of blue.

"What's the matter?" she inquired, seeing at once that something was troubling Uncle Henry.

"What *ain't* the matter?" the old fellow screamed, but glad of someone to whom he could unburden his overflowing heart. "Gol darn it! By gollies! I got it again!" he cried, seized with another inspiration. He eyed the radiant Lucia, as a miser might appraise a new gold coin. "Mis' Pell," he said, twirling his chair so that he caught a better glimpse of her.

"Yes?" she said, half-way down.

"You and Gil's old friends, ain't you?" The question was as direct as anything could be.

"Yes," was the equally direct answer.

"Want to do him a good turn?" asked the scheming old man.

"Of course. What do you mean?" She was at his side now.

"He's got a chance to make a swell marriage," announced Uncle Henry.

"What?" There was a curious catch in Lucia's voice.

"A rich marriage," Uncle Henry went on, almost smacking his lips over the words.

Lucia went over to the window, so that she would not face the invalid.

"Not as rich as yourn, of course," Uncle Henry pursued; "but rich for him - and he won't do it." He waited for her to say something; but she did not speak. There was a pause. Lucia looked out at the baking valley, and off to the far mountains, and the ticking of the clock could be heard like steady rain in a cistern. Then she went over to the table near the alcove, where a few books were scattered about. She opened one, and pretended to read. All the time Uncle Henry's eyes never left her. And she knew he was searching her thoughts.

"He won't?" she finally said.

"No - the gol darn fool!" the old fellow screamed again.

"Does he - does he love her?" Lucia brought herself to ask.

Quick as a flash Uncle Henry came back: "Sure he does! It's the only thing for him to do. He ain't got no right to be livin' alone. All he don't get skinned out of he gives away. Never gets nothin' to eat. If ever a feller needed a nice, sensible wife to take care of him, it's Gil. I know. Ain't I his uncle?"

"You think she would - make him - a good wife?" Lucia Pell got the words out somehow, never lifting her eyes from the printed page.

"The finest in the world!" Uncle Henry affirmed. "Now, looky here, Mis' Pell: He won't listen to me - funny the way folks are about their relatives. But I was thinkin' that mebbe if you was to ask him -"

Lucia was startled. "I?" she said.

The wheel chair bobbed about. "Yes. You and him bein' old friends that way, mebbe he'd pay some attention to you. Make him see what a gol darn fool he is and give him h -. Give it to him good! It's a wonderful chance. He'll never get another. Darned if I see how he ever got this. But he has. And what we gotter do is to make him take it." He paused; but she said nothing. He waited a moment. Then, - "What do you say? Will you?"

"You - think he should?"

"I know darn well he should!"

Lucia closed the book and put it down. She looked straight at Uncle Henry. "I should think he would see it for himself."

Uncle Henry showed his disgust - not for her, but for his nephew. "Aw, he's always been like this. I remember five or six years ago, he told me then he wouldn't ask no woman to marry him until he got a lot of money. False pride, I call it. What'd the world come to if everybody felt like that?"

"You think it's only pride that's keeping him from it?" Her voice was very low.

"Well, what else could it be, I'd like to know."

"Maybe it's because he hasn't a lot of money. He may be honest in that."

"Well, mebbe you're right. That may be it. What do you say?"

"All right," Lucia Pell said. But she turned away.

Uncle Henry was delighted. "That's the idee! Hooray!" Had he been able to stand, he would have risen and given three rousing cheers. He hadn't been so happy in years. "We'll put it over yet, by heck!"

He hadn't seen his nephew come into the room, with a ball of stout twine in his hands.

"Put what over?" Gilbert asked.

Uncle Henry was taken aback, but he quickly covered his confusion.

"Oh, somethin'. It's a secret." He turned and addressed Lucia Pell. "Don't forget," he admonished, and swiftly wheeled himself out into the yard again.

CHAPTER VI

WHEREIN AN OLD LOVE AWAKENS, PELL REVEALS HIS TRUE COLORS, A MORTGAGE IS ABOUT TO BE FORECLOSED, THE CONTENTS OF A SATCHEL ARE MADE KNOWN, UNCLE HENRY SPRINGS A SENSATION, AND PELL TAKES AN OPTION

Lucia's eyes were following Uncle Henry's heaving chair; for the yard was full of little stones, and the invalid bumped along, not always able to keep on a smooth track. She smiled as she watched him.

"What was he talking about?" Gilbert asked, kneeling on the floor, and folding one rug that had slipped away.

"Oh, nothing," Lucia Pell answered. "You know how old people babble on sometimes about nothing." She turned and looked at him. Still the same handsome Gilbert! "What are you doing?"

"Nothing. You know how young people go on doing nothing. I'm just rolling up these rugs and blankets. I'm going to send them away."

Lucia saw the beautiful pattern of one Navajo as Gilbert held it, unfolded, from the floor. She came over to him.

"You're sending them away - when they're so exquisite?" she asked. "This flaming one -" she picked it up and draped it around her. "Why, it's like the sunset. And you do have such beautiful sunsets here, Gil."

"I got them up especially, in honor of your visit," Jones said; and then he remembered how many times a remark like that must have been made, by many a lover, as if it were quite original, as if no one had ever thought of it before!

But Lucia took him seriously, dropped the wonderful blanket and went over to the door again. "I never grow tired of this view, Gil. It's almost as if God were an artist and had spilt the colors from His palette. And yet not that, quite. The colors are more like jewels. The morning's opals; the noon's pearls; the evening wears rubies in her hair. There's a sort of beauty that makes one ache. It seems to me sometimes as if I couldn't stand it - just the way the Grand Canyon got hold of me. Doesn't it affect you that way - you who have so much poetry in you?"

"Indeed it does, Lucia. I've often watched that sky until I've forgotten all about my cattle - both of them!" He laughed, and reached for the twine. He was always turning their serious moments into a jest. As long as she had been here with her husband, he kept at a distance.

Lucia saw his hand go out. "The string?" she said. "I'll get it." She left the door, and handed him the twine which he had put on the table.

"Thank you," said Gilbert. "Do you mind putting your finger - there? Never mind. I think I can do it, after all."

"Oh, do let me help you," she said. "I'd like to." And she leaned down, knelt beside him, and held her white forefinger on the cord.

How it happened, neither of them ever knew. But a sudden electric thrill ran through their veins. Something hammered in their brains. For a brief instant, their hearts beat as though the whole world must hear. He had touched her finger, and, before he was aware of it, he had dared to lean over and kiss it. Not a word was said - there was no time for words. They did not need speech to understand. It was the old, but ever new experience of the ages: two who loved each other had found out in the twinkling of an eye - and she belonged to another. There was a moment of terrible silence. Then,

"I'm sorry," was all Gilbert could get out.

"But you touched my hand many a time, in the old days," Lucia said.

"That was different. You're married now. Oh, there is a vast change since then. I could not - Forgive me, my dear." He turned away his face. He did not want her to read what was in his eyes. "Shall I send them, or would you rather take them with you?" he asked, hiding behind that commonplace question the emotion he felt. His voice held a note of pain.

Lucia rose. "You mean you want to give these wonderful rugs and blankets to me? - these priceless things."

"More than that. I want you to have them - to remind you - sometimes of -" He broke off, like a frightened lad.

"As though I should ever need reminding! How dull you men can be! But I don't want to take them from you, Gil."

"I'm giving up this ranch," he told her, "I shan't want them any more. Please take them, for my sake." He made a gesture, as though they were the last of his poor possessions.

"I thought you loved it here?" she said.

"I do - in a way."

"Then why are you giving it up?" was the natural question.

Charles Hanson Towne

He hesitated, not knowing what to answer. "I thought I'd try something else for awhile. I hate to have to tell you this, Lucia; but the fact is, I - I've got to leave to-day. I was going to tell you before, only I was hoping that something might turn up at the last minute, and - well, it hasn't. That's all."

There was nothing she could say; and they stood looking at each other in silence - a silence that was far more eloquent than speech. Gilbert went over and sat on the case, and Lucia finally said:

"Then we won't see each other again?"

He nodded, sorrowfully. Lucia Pell went over to the door and looked out once more. He watched her, covertly - her every gesture held a new meaning for him now. The silence continued. At length she turned back and faced him. He could not stand it, and bent quickly over the rugs and blankets.

"I don't know what to say, Gil." She moved closer to him. "I've had a wonderful time - you know that. I want to thank you for it. You've been awfully kind to us."

"Having you here is all the thanks I want," he answered. He had everything snugly packed now.

"I'm glad we happened to meet again. Though it does seem strange, doesn't it, that we should run across each other after all these years!"

He stood up straight. "All these years! You talk as if you were a hundred!" And he tried to smile.

"I am - nearly," she laughed. "I'm twenty-four, you know."

"Really? It doesn't seem possible!"

"I was eighteen when you went away. And that's nearly six years ago. Time flies, doesn't it?" She smiled at her bromidic remark, and sat down; but he did not reply, "Gil," she said at last. He looked up. "Why didn't you come to see me before I went away?"

"I don't know. I suppose -"

"You went away from Maine without my knowing - without even coming to say good-bye. Was that fair, was that the thing for a man like you to do?"

How he wished she had not brought up these burning memories!

"I was broke, and I - " he managed to explain.

Lucia knew what he must be feeling now. She got up and went over to his side; she did not dare place her hand in his. Never must there be again that electric current between them. "But you're all right now, aren't you,Gil?"

He seemed abstracted, suddenly lost in another world. "Huh?" he uttered. Then, as if coming to himself, "Oh, my, yes! I'm doing splendidly now, Lucia!"

"I'm so glad, Gil. But you haven't answered my question yet."

"About my not coming to say good-bye?"

She nodded.

"It was pride, I suppose," he went on.

"Very foolish pride. And life is so short. You hurt me a great deal."

"I'm sorry. What more can one say? If I - "

"I thought I had done something to offend you," she said, standing very still, and looking far beyond him now, as though viewing their whole unhappy past. "And it's worried me even until this very day. I didn't do anything to offend you, did I, Gil?"

"You? You, Lucia?" he cried. "You couldn't do anything to offend me. Surely you must know that." He said it as a man says such things to the one woman he loves.

"It was only pride?" she was anxious to know again. "Because you were poor! Gil! Did you think so little of me as that?" There was a half-sob in her voice.

"I hoped to pick a fortune off a tree somewhere, and come back and surprise you with it. I was going to buy an automobile - one of those low ones as long as a Pullman car - and fill it with roses, and come dashing up to your front door and take you for a ride through the hills. It was to be autumn. I had even that fixed," he laughed. "Oh, I had everything thought out! And you were going to be so proud of me!... But I couldn't find a fortune-tree anywhere...." He looked away, embarrassed. He hadn't meant to tell her this.

"Gil!" she cried.

"I guess they don't grow any more. At least, not in this part of the country." He rose, a bit wearily, and walked over to the mantel-piece.

"What did you do, Gil?" she asked, her eyes following him.

"Well, I was a time-keeper on a railroad and weigh-boss in a coal mine. After that I punched cows until I got uncle to come here. Then the war started, and - that's all."

Then she asked what a woman always asks.

"Why didn't you ever write to me, Gil?"

"I was waiting for some good news to tell you. I felt you would consider me a failure - a rank failure. I couldn't have stood that. Women don't know how proud men are about that."

"Maybe we don't - and maybe we do, Gil." She went closer to him. "Why don't you marry?" she dared to inquire.

He was startled. "Marry?" he repeated.

"Yes; you need someone to take care of you - someone to look after your daily needs - every man does."

"I guess there's no doubt about that. But it ought to be a guardian in my case; or maybe a keeper." She could see that he was stalling for time, and trying to laugh off a topic that was serious indeed to him.

"We're such old friends, Gil," she said, looking at his handsome face. "I don't like to go - to think of you always, like this - alone."

"I still have uncle," he reminded her.

"Oh, don't joke, Gil! You need a woman - a wife - someone to mother you."

"All those?"

Why couldn't he be serious for a moment? She asked him that.

"I don't dare to, Lucia." His voice was low.

She was a bit puzzled. "Why?"

"Because the minute you begin to take life seriously, it takes *you* that way, and then -"

"But don't you see what it would mean to you, dear Gil? To have someone always here; to kiss you when you go; to greet you when you come back; to laugh with you when you are glad; and comfort you when things go wrong. To give you the sympathy, the understanding that a man finds only in a woman's heart. Don't you see, Gil?"

"Yes, of course I see," he said, his head bowed a little.

"Then why don't you, Gil? She'd make you very happy - a woman like that. I want you to understand."

"Don't you suppose I do? Don't you suppose I've always understood, ever since -"

"Ever since when, Gil? Then you have known such a woman?"

He moved his head.

"You have!...And you cared for her?"

He nodded again.

"You loved her?" she hurried on.

His voice was hoarse. "Yes." The monosyllable got out somehow.

"You still love her. I know it, I can see it. Who is she, Gil? I want to know."

"Don't you know?" he asked, and looked her straight in the eyes.

Before she could answer, there were footsteps outside, and Pell could be heard whistling. He rushed in now, the bag still clutched in his hand. At once he sensed something strange in their attitude, and he eyed both of them shrewdly, covertly, briefly. Not a word was uttered. He threw the bag on the table, as though he had noticed nothing, and in the most matter-of-fact tone said,

"Say, how about dinner?"

"It isn't ready yet," Gilbert informed him. Lucia took advantage of her husband's question to move over toward the door.

"Why, good God, man, it's nearly three o'clock! We're not on a hunger strike, are we?" And he laughed at his own dull witticism.

"I'll see about it now," Jones promised.

"Haven't got a drink, have you, while we're waiting? Not that I need an appetizer! And it's damned hot, I know, to guzzle whiskey."

"There's nothing good in the place. But I think the cook has some tequila."

"Tequila? What's that, Jones?"

"It's a Mexican drink."

"Has it got a kick in it?" the other wanted to know.

"I never heard anybody complain," Gilbert smiled. "After two or three of 'em, I never saw anybody able to complain!"

He started toward the kitchen.

"What does it taste like?" said Pell, detaining him.

"Oh, sort of like gasoline with bichloride of mercury in it," Jones answered his eager questioner.

"No wood alcohol?" suspiciously. Pell was always looking out for himself.

"Oh, it's safe enough, I assure you. Would you like to try some

Charles Hanson Towne

of it?" Gilbert suggested.

Pell thought a moment - but only a moment. "I'll try anything once, and anything to drink more than once - if I'm alive the second time."

His host smiled. "I'll get you some if there's any left," and went to the kitchen to see. He couldn't help wondering why a man like Morgan Pell, with so many responsibilities, should wish to drink tequila.

Left alone, there was that strange silence between Lucia and her husband which so often occurred nowadays. A barrier was between them, none the less real because it was invisible. She knew his moods so well, and she dreaded the things he might say, all his inhibitions gone, if he drank any of this deadly Mexican stuff. She would have halted Gilbert had she dared; but she knew that any such action on her part would have aroused Pell the more, inflamed him to anger; and, like most women of fine breeding, she dreaded a scene more than anything in the world. All that she said now was merely,

"I wish you wouldn't do that."

"Do what?" Pell asked, jerking out the two words in a high staccato. He hated to be questioned, particularly by his wife. His hands reached for the satchel he had brought in.

"Order a man around in his own house."

"And why not, I'd like to know?" Pell inquired. "Who's he, anyhow, and what difference does it make?"

Lucia remained perfectly calm. "Well, if you can't see, of course -"

"There's no use your trying to tell me. Is that what you were going to say?" His face showed his rage.

She did not answer. That infuriated him all the more.

"I see what you mean! But I don't agree," Pell pursued. "This Jones person is nothing in my life. And why I should be deprived of my liquor and forced to eat burnt beans three times a day, I can't see." He emitted a sound that might have been designated a laugh.

"But - while we -" Lucia started to argue, and then thought better of it.

"Why doesn't he set his liquor out and see that the meals are right, himself? Then there wouldn't be any need of my saying anything." His tone was brutally frank. He really disliked Jones, and would be glad when they could get back to New York. There was nothing here worth his consideration. Sturgis had been stupid to think so.

"But when we are enjoying his hospitality -"

"Enjoying? Ha! Suffering, I guess you mean!" And Pell's head went back and he gave out a guffaw.

Lucia waited for his false mirth to vanish. Then, "But you seemed very anxious to come here."

"Yes; because I thought he lived in a house, not a -"

The sentence was not completed; for Gilbert came back with a bottle of the deadly tequila in his hand.

"I'm terribly sorry," he apologized, "to have to tell you that dinner will be late."

"You mean later, don't you?" Pell edited the remark.

Gilbert handed him the bottle. "Maybe this will atone for the postponed banquet," he smiled. He got the water-bottle hanging on the peg by the fireplace, and brought that to Pell also. He tried to be as gracious as he could to anyone under his roof.

Pell took a swig out of the bottle - a long one. "Good God!" he exclaimed, his face almost purple, his brow puckered like a dwarf's.

"What's the matter?" Gilbert said. And he handed him the water-bottle.

"It's poison!" Pell cried. And as if he really believed it, and as though water were an antidote, he grabbed the water-bottle and drank from it swiftly and loudly. It was horrible the way he guzzled the liquid down. An animal would have done better.

"The Mexicans like their liquor strong," young Jones explained. "That's what's the matter with the cook."

Lucia was puzzled. "What do you mean?" she asked.

"Simply that he's been imbibing again. That's why dinner is so late. But we're getting used to it. There is nothing to do but stand it."

"Drunk?" Pell asked.

"Quite," answered Gilbert.

"Well, I don't know as you can blame him," Pell excused. "I'd be drunk too if I had to live here. What are you going to do about it?" He hung the water-bottle in its place on the peg.

"Red's trying to sober him up," Gilbert said.

They had had enough of the cook, Pell decided within himself. Dinner was inevitably late, and that was all there was about it. So he changed the subject abruptly.

"This ranch belongs to you, doesn't it?" he put the question direct to Jones.

"What's that?"

"I asked you," went on Pell, a little disconcerted at having to repeat his question, "if you own this ranch."

"I - er - yes. Why?" Gilbert said.

Pell was quick to notice the other's discomfiture. "I have a friend who thinks he wants to go into the cattle business. He asked me to look him up a place. It's his own money, of course."

"Then I'd advise him not to buy here," said Gilbert, much to Pell's amazement.

"Why?"

"It's too near the border," Jones answered. "The bandits come over and steal all your cattle. It's a rotten situation. I'm sorry I ever came down here."

"That makes it all the better," Pell was shrewd enough to say. "Then he'd lose his money quick, and be satisfied." And he laughed at what he thought a witticism.

Uncle Henry's wheel chair crossed the sill at that moment. His face was full of news. "Hardy's coming!" he informed those in the room.

"A man to see me on a matter of business," Gilbert remembered. "Will you excuse me?" He turned to Pell.

"But I want to talk to you myself," the latter reminded him.

But young Jones had gone to the door. "I'm sorry. This is imperative, and I must see him." He turned definitely as if to go.

"But I was here first," Morgan Pell argued. He hated to be beaten by this stripling.

"I regret that I must insist," Gilbert said. And there was a duel of eyes, as well as of wits, before Jones turned away, easily the victor. After all, it was his own house, his own ranch. His visitor was wise enough to realize that. He walked over to the table and took the tequila bottle up again. "I'll have another drink, if you don't mind," he said, to Gilbert's back.

"Drink?" yelled Uncle Henry from his chair, frantic at the thought of any more of their precious liquor being consumed. It was hard enough to get, even when one had plenty of money.

"Help yourself," said Gilbert, not a little ashamed of the protest in Uncle Henry's voice.

"While I'm waiting," Pell laughed; and, taking the bottle, he went out.

Uncle Henry could scarcely control himself. He switched his chair in his nephew's direction. "Say," he wanted to know, "have you been holding out on me?"

"It's only tequila," Gilbert tried to pacify him.

"I don't care if it's only varnish!" cried Uncle Henry, his voice rising high and shrill. "And you let him go and take the whole bottle!" He pounded the arm of his chair, always his last resort.

Gilbert paid no attention to him. He went over to the table, as though he hadn't said a word, and began looking for a letter in one of the drawers. Almost immediately he laid his hand on it, and, turning to Lucia, said:

"If you'll excuse me?"

"Certainly. I must go and pack anyway." And she started toward the steps that led upstairs.

Gilbert went through the alcove; and no sooner had his broad shoulders disappeared than Uncle Henry turned to Lucia Pell and cried:

"Hey! Wait a minute."

Lucia was astonished. She had one foot on the step, and she turned about to see if Uncle Henry was actually addressing her. There was, obviously, no one else to address; but she thought the cook must have come in when her back was turned. She glared at the invalid, and said nothing.

"Did you ask him?" Uncle Henry went on, paying not the slightest heed to her surprised glance.

"Ask who what?" Lucia asked. She was not a little interested now. She came back into the room.

"Ask him about marryin' - you know. I gotter find out because Hardy's comin'." No speech could have been plainer and balder. "Did you?"

Lucia was nonplussed at the old man's crude directness. "Yes - I mean no. I don't remember."

"Don't remember!" Uncle Henry yelled. "But that's what I left you here for! We had it all framed up! Why didn't you?"

Lucia's head drooped a bit. "We were talking about something else."

The crabbed man was inflamed by this reply. "What was you talkin' about that was so gol darned important that you forgot the only important thing there was to talk about?...Well?" he cried, when she said nothing. "By gollies! I remember now! You was the gal he wouldn't ask to marry him because he didn't have no money!" He did not notice that his nephew had come back from the other room just in time to hear this last remark. He went on relentlessly to Lucia: "And me like a poor boob forgettin' all about it until now!" He suddenly saw Gilbert, and, not a whit abashed, turned on him. "So that's why you won't marry Hardy's daughter! I see it all now! I've been as blind as a hoot-owl!"

There came the sound of a Ford stopping outside, and footsteps approached up the path that led to the adobe.

"It's all right, Lucia," Gilbert said, and she went upstairs, almost weeping. Then he whirled about and glared at his uncle. "It's a good thing - no, I don't know what I'm saying. You're an invalid, or I'd strike you, despite your years, Uncle Henry. For heaven's sake, can't you learn to mind your own business?"

"I ain't got any. You robbed me of it!" the old man flamed back. "Now I'll mind yours for a change. Make a monkey out o' me, will you, gol darn you!"

As he was starting for the door, he bumped directly into Jasper Hardy and his daughter Angela and the ubiquitous "Red." The trio had come over in the Ford.

Hardy, tall and thin, wore a funereal black coat, despite the heat, and a somber dark Stetson hat. He must have been fifty or more. His skin looked bloodless, and his eyes still had that hard, pale look. It was difficult to trust eyes like those. He ambled, rather than walked, and his lean, lanky legs would have made him a fortune on the stage. It was difficult to believe, as everyone always said, that the lovely little Angela, with her bright black eyes and her rose-red cheeks, was the daughter of this sinister man. She was as attractive as a rose; - a typical frontier maiden, romantic, emotional, peppery when occasion demanded - just the kind to take the fancy of an honest soul like "Red." His eyes followed her wherever she went, as ever. She could not sit down or stand up or open her delicate lips but that he stared at her, hoping he could be of some service to her. Sometimes he prayed that some slight accident would befall her in order that he might prove his devotion. If she would only be sent to jail, that he could bring her soup and pass it through the bars of her cell! He dreamed this once, and awakened in a cold perspiration; for Angela (in the dream) realized his worth then; and the Governor pardoned her, and they were married at once and lived happily ever afterward. A Freudian lapse, maybe, and a dream a little too sane, according to the psychologists, to mean anything much; but rich in hidden meanings for poor "Red." Oh, that it would come true! She had been so kind and sweet to him this morning.

Hardy ambled into the room, and looked around in the most casual way. His eye lit upon Uncle Henry first of all, naturally; for he had all but bumped into him.

"How are you, Smith?" he said. "Evenin'."

And Angela piped up, to both uncle and nephew: "Good evening."

Gilbert bowed. "How do you do? Won't you sit down?" And he pulled out a chair for Angela.

"No, thanks," Hardy said; but

"Yes, thanks!" his daughter decided, and popped into a seat. "Red" loved her for it.

Hardy turned to young Jones. "Well?" was all he said. He referred to his state of health - not that he cared how Gilbert felt.

"Anything but," the latter answered.

Jasper Hardy always went right to the point. He disliked equivocation; so he rasped out immediately:

"Have you got the money?"

"No."

Angela, who was tender-hearted, tried to intercede.

"Now, father!" she pleaded. She hated this business.

But Hardy paid not the slightest heed to her. He was a man of action, and women shouldn't interfere - particularly young and pretty girls.

"Then I reckon I'll have to foreclose," he went on relentlessly. "There's nothing else to do." His hands closed tightly, and his hard eyes looked even harder.

"I'm afraid you're right," Gilbert said. "I was afraid it would be inevitable. I couldn't have hoped for anything else."

"I'm sorry," Jasper Hardy announced; but did not mean it.

Gilbert told him so. "Moreover, I know how you got your money," the young man was not afraid to say.

"I know how he got mine, gol darn it!" Uncle Henry cried. Hardy glared at him, seemed to smite him with his eyes.

"I'm not in business for my health," he said coldly.

"Nor for anybody else's," Uncle Henry, unabashed, told him.

Angela feared there was going to be trouble. "Now, daddy, you mustn't - you really mustn't - I feel -"

But her father did not hear her.

"The time's up at eight o'clock," was all he said, and looked sternly at Gilbert, much as a judge who is pronouncing sentence looks at the prisoner at the bar.

"I know it," said Gilbert.

"Now, daddy -" Angela began again.

Hardy was angry at her repeated solicitation. "Will you let me alone? This is my business," he said to her in a firm voice, "Remember that, and don't attempt to put your finger in the pie. This is my business, I tell you."

"Yes, I know daddy; but you needn't be so mean about it."

"I'm a plain man, and I don't believe in beating about the bush. Get that through your head - every one of you, I mean."

"But you might at least be - " his daughter began once more.

"Won't you please keep still?" His rage was mounting; and his brow darkened.

"I only want you to be nice about it, daddy," Angela persisted, sweetly.

"How can anybody be nice about a thing like this?" said the man of iron.

"I know I could be," Angela informed him.

Her father looked at her. "Well, what would you do?"

"Give him his ranch back, of course!"

Jasper Hardy couldn't believe what he had heard, and from his own child. "Well, for the love of heaven!" he cried, and almost burst out laughing.

"We've more ranches now than we know what to do with. Everybody is aware of that."

Here was Uncle Henry's chance. "That's the idea!" he cried.

"What do you want it for, anyhow?" But no one paid any attention to him.

"Oh, will you, daddy - for my sake?" Angela pleaded.

Hardy was adamant. "Certainly not! What a stupid request. How did such ideas come into your head?"

"But I don't see why -" the unremitting Angela started to say.

Her father was furious now, and tired of her prattle. He turned to "Red." "Take her out doors, will you?" as though she were a child.

"Red's" face gleamed as if a lantern had been lighted behind it. He turned eagerly to Angela. "*Will* I!" he cried.

But Angela was scornful. How foolish of "Red" to think her father could dismiss her in this way! She proceeded as though no such suggestion had been made, and addressed her father once more, not in the least perturbed:

"Of course, if you're going to be nasty about it -" Then, sweetly, to Gilbert she continued: "Please don't think too badly of us, Mr. Jones. Father doesn't really mean any harm."

"No more'n a rattlesnake," Uncle Henry leaned out of his chair to whisper in a voice that could be heard by everyone.

"It's just that he doesn't know any better," Angela went on to Gilbert. "He's really very neighborly when he wants to be."

She rose, and "Red" offered her his arm; but she haughtily rejected it, and went out the door, unaware that the devoted and humble "Red" followed her.

Jasper Hardy was glad she had gone. He could speak freely now. He addressed Jones.

"Packed up yet?" he inquired, sarcastically, as though he meant to intimate that his coming journey would be a pleasant one.

Gilbert could have struck him; but he replied quietly: "I'll just put on my hat and I'll be ready."

But the literal-minded Hardy remarked:

"Them crockery, and the rugs?" pointing to the articles significantly.

"The rugs I'm presenting to a friend of mine. The crockery goes to the cook. He has a family, you know." His irony was lost on the imperturbable Hardy, who merely asked:

"And you ain't got anything more to say, Jones?" He watched him closely.

"Nothing of general interest."

But Uncle Henry wasn't going to let matters end here.

"I've got something to say," he announced like an oracle. "Your daughter wants to marry him!" He imagined this would prove a thunderbolt; but Hardy calmly asked:

"How do you know that?"

"Because she told me, that's how! And if only the gol darn fool would do it like I want him to -" He addressed himself suddenly to his nephew, who now stood on the other side of the table: "Aw, come on. Be a good feller, won't you?"

Again this outlandish interfering on the part of Uncle Henry! Was the old fellow losing his reason? There was no privacy in their affairs - everything was an open book to anyone who came to the adobe. It was getting to be unbearable. Gilbert had controlled himself long enough in the presence of others. He was sick and tired of the old man's meddling.

"Keep still!" he warned him, and shook his finger in his face, "Keep still, I say!" His cheeks were scarlet with rage. The blood pounded in his veins.

The invalid never lost his courage. "You won't marry her?" was what he said.

"How can I, you - you -" Gilbert could scarcely stand it any longer.

"Gol darn, the gol darn -" cried Uncle Henry; and then he swerved on Jasper Hardy: "Maybe you can persuade him," he suggested.

"Persuade him to what?"

"To marry her," Smith brazenly said.

"I don't want him to marry her," the father was honest enough to say.

This had never occurred to Uncle Henry. "What's the matter with him?" he asked, his eyes opening wide in amazement.

"It would take too long to tell you." Hardy considered the argument closed; but Uncle Henry came right back again:

"But he's my nevyer!"

"That's one of my main reasons," Hardy cruelly announced; and the only come-back poor Uncle Henry had was an exasperated, "Oh, is that so!" drawled out peevishly, weakly.

"I want his ranch, not him," Hardy went on. He might have been discussing someone not in the room.

"But he's a fine young feller, if I do say so!" Uncle Henry came to Gilbert's rescue, after the manner of all relatives when an outsider steps in with criticism.

"Only a minute ago I heard you call him a gol darn fool!" Hardy triumphantly reminded him.

"There you are," said Gilbert, addressing his uncle. "That's what you get -"

"Do you think I want my darter to marry a gol darn fool?" Hardy fired back at the old man.

Uncle Henry was flabbergasted, completely done for, for the moment. "Well, what the -" But he could get no farther.

Jasper Hardy looked at Gilbert, "Well, now that's settled."

Uncle Henry butted in once more. "You won't let her?"

"Let her what?" A pair of steely eyes were fixed on the questioner.

"Marry him. Won't you?"

"Of course not. What are you talking about, you old fool?"

Uncle Henry was not to be outdone. He whisked around, facing the door, and called at the top of his voice:

"Angely! Angely!"

From the yard came back, "Yes, I'm coming!" and Hardy's daughter ran in, with "Red" at her heels.

"Did you call me?" she wanted to know, looking at all three.

"Yes; I did," said Uncle Henry. "I wanted to tell you that it ain't no use. They won't neither of 'em do nothin'."

"Who won't?" asked Angela, mystified. She hadn't an idea what the old man was talking about.

"The poor stiffs!" said Uncle Henry.

"Do what?" Angela pursued.

"I asked 'em!" the invalid whined.

The girl grew impatient. "For goodness' sake, asked them what?"

"To marry you, of course!"

Angela thought she must be dreaming.

"You - asked him - to marry me?" She looked about her, bewildered.

"Yes; and he turned you down!"

Surely now this must be a dream! "Red," too, was in a daze, suffering vicariously for his adored one.

"Oh!" cried Angela, when a full realization of what Uncle Henry meant came over her.

Uncle Henry went on: "Like your own payrent - the stony-hearted old reptile!"

"Oh, Gil -" began Angela in tears.

"Go on - you ask 'em!" suggested Uncle Henry.

"Gil -" the girl got out the first syllable of his name, and no more; for her little handkerchief was at her pretty nose.

"I'm sorry," said Gilbert, gallantly, going to her. "Please don't feel badly about it."

"Don't - don't speak to me!" Angela sniffed, and stamped her dainty foot. "Don't look at me! I hate you! I hate you! I hate you all!" Blinded with rage and tears, she crossed the room, and stumbled directly into Uncle Henry's chair, and all but tipped him over. "Red" followed her, solicitously.

"Now, Angela -" he said, and tried to grasp her arm. "Remember, I'm here!"

But all the thanks he got was a wild, "Get out of my way!" and he found himself pushed aside, into a corner. Another of her unsuspected tantrums!

"My God!" ejaculated Uncle Henry, furious at Angela's accident, which so directly concerned himself, "but everybody's unreasonable to-day!" He turned harshly on his nephew. "You make me sick, you! Here am I doing my gol darndest to save the mess you've made, and you won't even -" He broke off, unable, in his wrath, to continue. His eye lit on Hardy. "Look here," he cried, in desperation, "ain't there no way out of this thing? It was my money that bought this ranch, you know. And everybody knows it! The last ten thousand dollars I had in the world!" There was a sob in his voice on the last words.

Hardy looked at him, but with no pity in his gaze. "That's your lookout, Smith. Everybody for himself - that's my motto."

"And you'd throw me, old and sick, a invalid, out into the streets?" Uncle Henry whined. No one could get more pathos into his tones than Uncle Henry when he wanted to do so.

"No; I'd let you wheel yourself out," Jasper Hardy, again the literal-minded Hardy, said. It was one of the meanest remarks that even he had ever made.

"Say, ain't you got no heart at all?" Uncle Henry wanted to know.

"I used to have; but it cost me too much money," was Hardy's explanation and vindication. "Sentiment? Bosh!" And he made a gesture of deep disgust.

Uncle Henry wanted to put a curse on him! "Well, all I hope is that some day you'll go broke and they'll bounce you out into Main Street!" He chuckled in his chair.

"The line forms on the left," the imperturbable Hardy said. "You're the fifth that's had that hope this year. I don't care a rap what you think, old feller! Remember that!"

A shadow appeared on the doorsill; and Morgan Pell came in. His face was harder than ever. It was obvious that he had not thrown away the bottle of tequila until he had consumed the contents. His eye lit on Hardy at once, but he said nothing to him. Instead, he meandered toward Gilbert and observed, insolently enough:

"Look here, you've kept me waiting too long. What does this mean, eh?"

"I'm sorry," Gilbert returned. "I forgot all about you for the moment. Oh," he suddenly remembered that Hardy and Pell were unacquainted, "you two gentlemen ought to know each other. Mr. Pell, shake hands with Mr. Hardy."

Pell gave the other a curt nod. "How are you?" was all he could bring himself to say.

"Pleased to meet you," answered Hardy, and turned away, "Red" and Angela, interested spectators of this foolish proceeding, sat together on the little settee by the window near the door, and smiled at the shillyshallying of two grown men who should have known better. Civilization! A mockery, surely, when two men couldn't be amenable in the presence of others - two men who apparently had no reason for treating each other this way.

Pell suddenly addressed Jones. "I forgot to tell you that we're going this afternoon."

"I'm sorry," said his host.

"And before I go," Pell went on, "there's a matter of business I want to talk over with you. So if this gentleman is through -" he indicated Hardy with his thumb.

"Oh, I'll be through, all right - at eight o'clock to-night!" Jasper Hardy announced, and drew several silver dollars out of his trousers pocket and rattled them about in his hand, significantly.

"What do you mean, eight o'clock?" Pell wondered.

Hardy's eyes pierced him through and through. "When I foreclose the mortgage I hold on this ranch. Understand now?"

"When you foreclose...." Pell repeated the words as if he had not quite comprehended. Then he said to young Jones: "You said this ranch belongs to you?" What was the matter with him? Was his mind clouding? The stuff he had drunk? He put his hand to his forehead.

"It does," Gilbert explained. "You see, it isn't eight o'clock yet." A faint smile came to his lips.

Hardy failed to see the humor of the situation. "It's as good as eight o'clock, as far as he's concerned." And he rattled the silver coins again.

"Oh, is that so?" said Pell, beginning to see daylight. To young Jones he said: "How far is it to town?"

"Twenty miles, I should say."

Pell thought a second, "Is that flivver of yours working, Jones?"

"In a way."

Pell thought harder. "We've got plenty of time," he said, as if to himself. "Five hours! Get your hat," turning to the young man.

Gilbert was confused. "What's the idea?"

"We're going to pay the mortgage, of course. How much is it?"

"Shouldn't you have asked that first - as a good business man?"

"Answer me: how much is it?"

"Ten thousand dollars," came the quick response.

"And your equity?" Pell pursued, businesslike enough now.

"Another ten thousand."

He thought Morgan Pell would be stunned. Instead, he merely said, "I'll give you twenty thousand. That'll pay the mortgage and give you your ten back. You can give me an option while I'm arranging payment. Get me? That'll save time."

"You mean you'll give me twenty thousand dollars for this ranch?" Gilbert said, unable to understand.

"Exactly. Will you take it?"

"You bet your life he'll take it!" cried Uncle Henry, whom everyone had forgotten in the excitement of the moment. He rolled his chair expertly to the table, and peered into his nephew's face, fearing he would make a fool of himself once more. He was trembling with excitement.

"Then that's settled," Pell announced.

Unnoticed, Lucia had come to the top of the stairway, and stood listening to every word. And Hardy, who had been trying his best to get a word in edgewise, finally managed to cry out:

"Wait a minute!"

No one paid any attention to him. Gilbert was in deep meditation. He turned to Pell. "But I don't want to be under any obligation to you," he said.

"You won't," the other affirmed, and anxiety was in his voice. "Well, is it a go?"

"A go?" yelled Uncle Henry, unable to restrain himself. "It's gone!"

Hardy stepped in between Pell and Jones.

"Hold on, there! You can't do this."

Pell looked him squarely in the face, "Why not, I'd like to know."

"You mean you'd do me out of this property at the last minute?" Jasper Hardy asked.

Pell smiled. "That's my specialty!"

Indignation was in every fiber of Hardy's gaunt frame. He was losing his temper, and he was wise enough to know that that would never do. The unforgivable sin was to lose control of oneself. He must hold on to his voice, his movements; but a nest of hornets, under attack, could not have been angrier. "I protest!" he said, as calmly as he could. "Here I been settin' around waitin' for this place for five years! You can't come here an' take it away from me like this! No, sir, I won't have it!"

"Look here," Gilbert stepped in and said. "You're getting your money! What are you boiling about?"

"Red" had been listening attentively. He came close to Gilbert

Charles Hanson Towne

now, and said, "He wants the place. Didn't he just say so?"

"The place?" Gilbert repeated. "What the devil does he want the place for?"

Pell was growing impatient. There was too much quibbling. "We're losing time. Come on, let's get things settled."

Jones, however, was not to be hurried. "But I want to know why he wants this place so much." His suspicions were thoroughly aroused.

No one had observed Uncle Henry, who had silently wheeled his chair about until he got to the table, where Pell had left his satchel long ago. Like a curious old woman he now picked it up, brazenly opened it, and exclaimed:

"Hey! What the Sam Hill!" and backed away; but not until he had dipped his hands into the bag.

"What's the matter?" Gilbert asked, turning.

"It's full o' dirt! Just dirt!" Uncle Henry cried, and glanced about to see the effect of his surprising information.

"Dirt?" Gilbert said, not understanding.

"Yes, look!" And the old man pointed to the bag.

"But whose bag is it?" Gilbert persisted.

Uncle Henry lifted a thin finger, and directed it to Pell. "His'n!" he said.

But Gilbert was still in a daze.

"But what in the world could anybody be taking specimens of the soil around here for?" he inquired, and then began to think.

"Just to show the character of the ground, to see what will grow best," Pell hastened to explain.

"But it won't grow nothin' - not even rocks, an' you know it," the occupant of the wheel chair said. Then a new thought came to him, and he shot out, "By golly, I got it! He's an oil man, ain't he?"

Pell, furious, cried, "Oh, shut up! You old busybody!"

"He wants to buy this ranch because there's oil here!" Uncle Henry went on, not dismayed in the least at the other's insult.

"Bah!" Pell scornfully ejaculated.

Gilbert's face was a study. His eyes went from one to another in the room. "Oil?" he said. "Oil?"

"Yes, an' that's why *he* wants it, too!" cried Uncle Henry, pointing to Hardy this time, "The big skin!"

Pell took up the satchel - the little bag that had caused such a big sensation - and walked over to Uncle Henry's chair.

"Why, you poor old dotard, there's no oil in these specimens. You can smell 'em yourself if you want to," he said. But there was something in his manner of the lady who doth protest too much.

"No, I can't," Uncle Henry was swift to deny. "My smeller's no good." He sniffed comically - as if that proved his point.

"Let *him* examine them, then," suggested Pell, holding the satchel out to Gilbert, who stood on the other side of the table.

But Gilbert said nothing. It was Uncle Henry who again blurted out:

"That don't prove nothin'. Mebbe he hasn't found the oil yet.

Charles Hanson Towne

But it's here! If it ain't, why should you be fightin' so hard to get this rotten place? Tell me that, will you? Nobody else ever wanted it - except this kindly neighbor of ours!" He glared at Hardy triumphantly.

Pell was silent. Gilbert came to himself.

"Oil!" he said. "Then this ranch, instead of being worth nothing, would be worth hundreds of thousand of dollars - maybe millions!" He had taken the bag from Pell's extended hand, and now turned in dismay and confusion to the window, and put the bag on a chair. What a world it was, and how terrible that every other man seemed to be a predatory animal, ready to spring upon his neighbor and wrest anything he had away from him. What a world, indeed! No wonder young men lost their faith and courage!

"Millions!" The word caught Uncle Henry's fancy and imagination. He rolled it over on his tongue again and again. "Millions!" He babbled it, he played with it. "Millions!"

"Yes!" Gilbert said. "Think of that!" He turned and faced the others once more.

"An' we're goin' to get skinned out of millions! Oh, my Gawd!" The poor old invalid wailed it out, and rocked himself in his chair. How he wished he could rise, step out on the floor and knock Pell and Hardy down! Why didn't his strong and husky young nephew do it? What was the matter with the present generation, anyhow? Wasn't there any red blood in it? If he had only been younger, and strong, able to fight for what he knew to be his rights! But here he was, tied down in a wheel chair, trapped, helpless, impotent.

Pell was getting nervous, "This is nonsense," he said. "There's no oil here."

During all this long harangue, Lucia had quietly come down the stairs, and now stood directly behind her husband.

"And this is why you were so anxious to come here," she said, very low; yet everyone heard her statement. "To dig around, and then, if you found oil, to try to buy this place! Oh, I thought better of you than that, Morgan! What a trick - what a dishonorable trick!" She shuddered away from him. She almost hated him in this revealing moment.

"And why not?" was all her husband said. "Hadn't I a right to look for oil here? Suppose it was on the place?"

"You wouldn't have told him if you had found it! You know you wouldn't," his wife shot back at him.

Pell glared at her, fury in the look. "What do you think I am? Crazy?" he argued.

"But that isn't honest!" Lucia fearlessly said. "It's as crooked as it can be! And you know it."

"But it's legal!" Pell fired back. "And what do I care - what does anybody care - so long as it's legal! Ha! the courts would be with me! Moreover, it's the way you get the clothes you wear and the food you eat, and all those jewels that you hang on yourself when you undress and go to the opera!"

As he spoke, angrily, he went over to the chair where Gilbert had left the satchel, seized it and threw it on the floor, as though its contents were a symbol of the money she tossed away.

There was no use replying to a man like Pell. Lucia knew that. He was indignant that she had seen through his treachery. Here he was, a guest of Gilbert Jones, eating at his table day after day, pretending to be his friend, and all the while he had been planning this! And she had seemed to be a part of it all. What must Gilbert think of her? What must everybody think of her?

It was Hardy who broke the tension.

Charles Hanson Towne

"Say," he wanted to know, "who's this woman, and what's she busting into this for? We've had enough of petticoats around here for one day, it seems to me."

Uncle Henry was swift to inform him. "I'll tell you who she is - she's his wife!" And he pointed to Pell. "But she loves *him*!" And he pointed to Gilbert.

It was as though a bomb had exploded. Terror came into Gilbert's eyes, and fury into Morgan Pell's.

"What's that?" the latter cried, aghast. As a madman might, he stared at Gilbert for an instant; then his gaze shot in the direction of his wife, standing so calm at the other side of the table.

Young Jones almost made up his mind, in that blinding moment, to choke Uncle Henry once for all, and have it done with. This was the last stroke, the final straw. He could stand it no longer. He stalked over to his uncle, and really intended to lay violent hands on him; but of course he could not. That defenseless old man, that pathetic figure seemed to wilt before his piercing eyes, seemed to shrivel and literally fall to pieces. In hot disgust, Gilbert could only cry out:

"How dare you! How dare you, I say! This is the crowning interference!" He had put his hands behind his back and braced his shoulders, fearing that he would not be responsibile for what he did.

Uncle Henry, seeing that he was safe, came back to the fray.

"Well, you *couldn't* marry her," indicating Lucia, "an' you *wouldn't* marry *her*," pointing to Angela. "I guess I got some right to protect myself, ain't I?"

"Protect yourself!" repeated Gilbert, cynicism in his tone. He turned his back on them all and moved to the window. His very shoulders revealed the mental struggle he was going through.

Morgan Pell's eyes, all this time, had never left his wife. He studied her countenance as a pathologist might that of a person thought to be insane, and Lucia almost gave way under his relentless analysis. "Red," seeing the turn affairs had taken, quietly drew his gun, and Angela, frightened, put her hands over her shell-like ears. If there was one thing she dreaded, it was a shot. She was trembling like a leaf. She closed her eyes. She knew that "Red," in his devotion to Gilbert, would not hesitate to kill Pell.

With an inscrutable expression, Morgan Pell murmured, "H'm!" Then he turned swiftly on Uncle Henry and asked, "You have proof, I suppose?"

"Proof?" cried Uncle Henry.

"Yes."

"My Gawd," the invalid fairly shrieked, "all you gotter do is look at 'em! I been watchin' 'em ever since you came."

At this, Gilbert honestly believed that Uncle Henry had lost his reason. Surely this was the insane delusion of a senile old man; and he said as much to Pell.

"Senile yourself!" cried Uncle Henry, mad through and through, feeling he was immune from any attack. "Gol darn you!"

So there was no shutting Uncle Henry up! Gilbert, in despair, turned to Pell. "You don't believe it! You can't believe it!" he said. "This is madness -"

Pell said not a word; he seemed to be in deep thought. Suddenly his whole manner changed, his voice as well, and he faced Gilbert frankly.

Charles Hanson Towne

"Certainly I don't believe it. My confidence in my wife is implicit."

The metamorphosis was unbelievable. At least Uncle Henry thought so.

"Well, I always heard that husbands was boobs!" he announced, sarcastically.

Angela at that instant opened her eyes and took her fingers from her ears. Enough time had elapsed, she thought, for the worst to have happened.

"Has it gone off yet?" she naively asked.

"Has what gone off?" from Pell.

"Why, the gun, of course!" Angela replied.

"Gun?"

She looked at "Red." "He had one, and I thought maybe he'd shoot you, or maybe you'd shoot Gilbert, or maybe - Aren't you going to shoot him?"

"What for?"

"I thought that was what husbands always did!"

Pell smiled. "Not sensible husbands, my dear." Then he faced Gilbert again. "To go back to where we were: I will admit that there is a possibility of oil in this property. But it is only a possibility." The strain was broken. Everyone looked relieved. Lucia moved for the first time - she had been like a frightened bird under the spell of a serpent. "I'm a business man," Pell went on, suavely. "I'm willing to gamble twenty thousand dollars."

"You will?" cried Uncle Henry. There was no quieting him.

His life was one long question-mark.

"It's a fair proposition, and, as far as I can see, your only way out, Jones." He had paid no attention to the old man's interruption. But the latter broke in once more:

"Why don't you lend *us* the ten thousand and let *us* gamble?"

Pell was in no wise disconcerted by the query. He replied with another question - always the shrewd man's way out of a difficulty, "Would you, in my place?"

"Sure I would!" came from the wheel chair.

"Oh, you would -"

"Yes, *sir*!"

Pell had nothing further to say to him, but addressed himself to Gilbert again.

"However, if you don't think that offer fair, I'll give you twenty thousand cash and assume the mortgages."

"Twenty thousand?" Uncle Henry's eyes opened wide.

"Well, what do you say?" Pell wanted to know, still addressing Gilbert. He had no taste for Smith's constant interruptions.

But Hardy broke in, confounded by this talk. He saw himself slipping out of the transactions. "If you think you're going to..."

Pell paid no heed to what he said. "If I were in your place," he remarked to young Jones, "it wouldn't take me long to decide. You see, from me you get twenty thousand dollars clean. Otherwise, the place goes to him." He nodded toward Hardy. "And you get nothing. It's mighty plain - as plain as the nose on your face. I'm a plain man, and I don't quibble. I've made

Charles Hanson Towne

you a direct offer. Nothing could be fairer. Well?"

Gilbert didn't pause or hesitate a second. "All right. Give him the ten thousand," indicating Hardy.

Morgan Pell was visibly relieved. Things seemed to be going his way, just as he had planned. Sturgis had been right, after all. He rubbed his hands in satisfaction, "And now, to facilitate matters," he said, "if you will give us a ten-day option on the place, at a purchase price of thirty thousand..." He went to the table, and arranged pen and paper, and motioned Gilbert to be seated and write.

The latter was in the chair at once. "Thank you, no. Twenty," he said, and began to write.

"Twenty?" Pell repeated, and stroked his chin. He must be wary; he must go cautiously with this young fellow. He would see through him if he didn't. "Certainly. Your first offer is the one I take," Gilbert said in a firm voice.

Uncle Henry couldn't believe what he was hearing. "You mean you ain't going to take the other ten?" he cried, in surprise. Gilbert never looked up from his writing. The pen was moving swiftly over the paper. Uncle Henry was on the verge of a nervous breakdown then and there. He looked at Pell, eagerly. "Give it to me! *I'll* take it!"

But Pell only said: "Mr. Jones is the owner of this property," and watched the young man write.

Angela, like a timid bird, watched the proceedings breathlessly, and moved over close to her big father and put her little hand in his arm, "Isn't there anything we can do, dad?" she inquired.

Hardy pressed her fingers, and said, in a whisper: "But I'm not sure there's oil here. I'm not sure at all."

"But *he* seems to be," said the shrewd Angela, looking at Morgan Pell with his wily countenance.

"Oh, these New York fellers!" Hardy deprecated. "You never can tell!"

Gilbert rose.

"Finished?" asked Pell.

"Quite." And young Jones handed him the option on the property.

CHAPTER VII

WHEREIN LUCIA SEES TREACHERY BREWING, PELL PROVES HIMSELF A BRUTE, AND AN UNEXPECTED GUEST APPEARS

When Lucia saw Gilbert pass the paper to her husband, she thought she could not stand it. It was not her concern; and yet it was. Vitally, whatever affected young Jones affected her. She could not see him tricked, duped. And she knew that he was being played with, made a fool of. Some ulterior motive lay beneath this seeming generosity. She tried to control herself; but suddenly she found herself speaking.

"No! Don't! I can't -"

But she could get no farther. Something seemed to choke her, and make it impossible for her to continue.

Her husband looked at her in amazement. She turned away, and was silent.

"Thank you," said Pell to Gilbert. Then, to his wife he said: "And now that this is settled, we shall proceed to other business of even more importance. This gentle soul," looking at Uncle Henry, "has said that our friend loves you and that you love him. Is it true?" He was perfectly calm.

Once more he was the crafty, cruel, scheming man; and back into his eyes came that glitter she so feared.

Gilbert, astonished, got to the other side of the table.

"I thought we were through with all that!" he said. "What's the use of harping on it?"

"You were wrong," answered Pell, coldly. "I am a business man, as I told you before. I do one thing at a time." His lids half closed, his hands clenched. He swerved abruptly on his wife. "Well?" he said. "Well?"

"You mean to say," said Gilbert, "that you took seriously what my doddering old uncle said? I told you I thought he was crazy, and you seemed to agree with me. What are you talking about now?"

Morgan Pell's steel-gray eyes fastened themselves on Jones, "I am talking to my wife. I am not ready for you - yet. One thing at a time, you know." He looked again at Lucia. "Well? I am waiting. Answer me: Do you love him?"

Alarm at Pell's manner was rife in the room. What a brute he was, and how terrible was his verbal attack!

Lucia could not trust herself to speak. She knew she would have to reply to her husband's question, and though she knew her answer would be but a monosyllable, she could not get it out.

"Well?" Pell repeated, and the word was like a hammer-blow.

"No!" Lucia managed to say.

The husband now turned on Gilbert. "Do *you* love *her*?" he asked with great deliberation, as though he had rehearsed it in his mind for days.

"Certainly not," was the immediate reply.

The silence that followed could have been cut with a knife.

Everyone stood as though turned to stone. Surely this denial would be enough. Pell did not move. A menacing expression came over his face. As though there were no one else in the world, he glanced first at his wife and then at Jones, and affirmed with quiet deliberation:

"You're a couple of rotten liars!"

Had he been struck in the face, Gilbert could not have been angrier. He saw it all now - he was in this man's power, utterly. It had been planned craftily, smoothly. And there was no escape for Lucia. God! what he had gotten her in for! He cursed the tongue of Uncle Henry, and mentally he heaped maledictions on his own head for his gross stupidity. So this was how the land lay - this was the path that led to his destruction - ah! Not only his, but hers! Angry as he was, he knew it would be futile to do anything but try, even now, to placate this wretched specimen of a man. He had to think quickly. There was not an instant to lose.

"But you said you didn't believe..." he began; but Pell came mercilessly back at him!

"I didn't - then. The time was inopportune."

Uncle Henry clutched the arms of his chair. "Ooooooh! The dirty bum!" he yelled.

Pell went on, inexorably. "But now that she herself has admitted it, and -"

"Admitted it!" Gilbert cried, his rage now at the boiling point.

"Yes! By everything she has said and done to-day. My dear fellow," with a subtle change of tone, "God knows I am no prude." He smiled a bland smile. "But there are limits to what any husband can endure." His lips became thin and terrible; his eyes were gleaming slits.

Gilbert was aghast. He saw no solution of this painful situation; no safety for Lucia - his thoughts were all of Lucia.

"You don't think that!" he said, "You couldn't possibly think that! Oh, my God!"

Morgan Pell sneered at him. "I know what I would have done, in your place and with your opportunities."

Gilbert found it hard to realize that any husband could say a thing like this in the presence of his wife. It revealed, if anything further were needed to reveal, the cur in the man.

"We're not all as rotten as you are, Pell! Don't forget that!" he cried. "You're a dog - a low-down dog." It was all he could do not to spring upon this craven and pin him to the floor.

"And we're not all as discreet as you!" Pell flung back. "And now, if you don't mind," he added insinuatingly, "I'd like to talk to my wife - alone."

Gilbert was consumed with fear for Lucia. "What?" he cried.

"Have you any objections?" Pell said, curling his lip. The irony in his tone was unmistakable.

Gilbert moved toward the door. "Why - no."

"Thank you," Pell said; and he threw wide the door leading from the alcove so that his host might pass through. He waited for him to do so. Gilbert hesitated for the fraction of a second. He looked at Pell, and then at Lucia, still lovely for all her suffering. There was nothing to say - nothing he could say. He disappeared into the other room, and shut the door behind him. Pell immediately turned to the others. "Well?" he said.

"You mean you want us to get out too?" Uncle Henry asked, indignation in his high voice.

Charles Hanson Towne

"That's exactly what I do mean," Morgan Pell stated, firmly. "And the sooner the better."

The situation, he felt, was entirely in his hands.

"Oh, very well!" Uncle Henry replied. He pushed his chair toward the door, murmuring as he went, "Thank God I ain't his wife! That's all I got to say!"

Hardy was still standing in the shadows. He looked at "Red." "What's he going to do?" meaning Pell.

"I don't know. I -" the foreman answered. Angela, frightened, followed the husky "Red" through the door; and the husband and wife were left entirely alone.

There was a pregnant silence. Terror came into Lucia's heart. Her brain reeled. She had seen Morgan in a temper before - many times; but never with quite this sinister light in his eyes, this tense, quiet force behind his slightest gesture. What was he going to say to her? She felt like an animal at bay. She determined that she would gain one advantage by making him be the first to speak. But as he approached her slowly, fear seized her. He seemed no longer a man, just a hulking giant - a brutal, frenzied creature; and something quite apart from herself caused her to cry out:

"What are you going to do?" Oddly there flashed into her mind that very line, and she wondered where she had heard it. Yes, even in her terror, her abject fear, she remembered. It was once when, as a child, she had seen a dramatization of "Oliver Twist." Bill Sykes came toward Nancy, just as Morgan was coming toward her now, with leering countenance, and the poor wretch had screamed out: "What are you going to do?" That scene was forever photographed on her brain, and now, from some strange recess, Nancy's pitiful words came back to her.

He did not answer. Another step, and he would be upon her.

"What is it, Morgan? Oh, what is it?" She shrunk back, slowly. If he touched her...

But he did not lift his hand, as she fully expected him to do. Instead, he uttered only two words. They were a command.

"Kiss me!"

Almost she would rather have felt his blows raining on her head.

"What?" she cried, a new amazement within her.

He glared down at her. His breath was on her cheek.

"You heard," he stated. And he stood stock still.

Frightened beyond believing or seeing, she offered her cheek to him. "But I -" she managed to get out.

Pell saw that she was shrinking away again; she could not bring herself to do as he willed.

"So!" her husband cried, significantly. Now she realized, in a blinding flash, the cruel subtlety behind his test of her. Her head went back; she closed her eyes. And then - how she did it she never knew - she raised her mouth.

"I don't want to kiss you." It was the refinement of cruelty. "I want *you* to kiss *me*. Do it!" His hands were behind his back. He stood straight and stiff as an Indian chief.

He watched her least movement. He put his lips very close to her mouth. She struggled in that one mad second, and tried to kiss him. She could not - she could not bring herself to the act.

He laughed sardonically. The devil himself could not have laughed liked that.

"Some women could have done it," he told her, sternly. "But not you, my dear...." Fury and sarcasm were in his tone. "So! That's it, is it? And I stand blindly by while you and he..."

Utter madness seemed to rush upon him.

Lucia had backed to the table. "No! I can't. You - you brute!"

Pell watched her, steadily. "Do you think I am a fool? Or that you are more than human?" he cried out.

"I swear to God!" she contradicted him.

"Ha! You've had your turn, my lady! Now, it's mine! And after all I've done for you, you ungrateful hussy!"

The clock struck three. It seemed an eternity until the little bell ceased. Her life with him swam before her in that brief period. All she could utter was:

"What are you going to do?" And she clutched her hands in helplessness, for she read some sinister purpose in his voice.

"I'm going to do what I once saw another sensible husband do under these circumstances."

Lucia's face was ashen now. "What is that?"

A second's pause. She hung on his answer.

"Horses don't know who they really belong to. So they are branded. There is no reason why women equally ignorant shouldn't be similarly treated." Every word was measured, uttered with fearful distinctness. His hand shot behind him on the table, where "Red" had left his spurs. Lucia saw the swift movement.

"No!" she screamed, "Oh, no, Morgan, not that!" Her senses reeled. The earth crashed beneath her.

But he paid no heed. He seized her fiercely by one arm, reaching far out to do so, and, gorilla-like, he had her, this weak flower, in his clutches. He pinioned her deftly, and thrust her lovely body back, until her face looked upward from the table. With his right hand, he started to tear her beautiful face to shreds with the cruel spurs, forever to ruin her glorious features, when, as if through a miracle, the door was thrown wide open, and a strange figure stood on the sill - a Mexican in a great sombrero, a flaming red kerchief at his throat, and eyes that gleamed and glistened, teeth that were like the whitest ivory.

He stood, with arms crossed, surveying the scene. If lightning had struck the adobe, Pell could not have been more dazed.

He released his wife. "What the devil!" he cried. "Who are you?"

"Hold up your hands!" yelled the bandit, stepping over the threshold. And Pell's hands went up, like magic, the spurs jangling to the floor.

There was a noise without, and Uncle Henry was pushed in by a crude, foul-looking Mexican, then came "Red," Angela, and Hardy, followed by another Mexican bandit, and several Mexicans.

"Who is he? What does this mean?" Pell cried out.

"This is Pancho Lopez!" "Red" Giddings said. Everyone's hands were lifted, and pistols were held by the Mexicans, ready to go off at the slightest sign of rebellion.

"Pancho Lopez?" Pell repeated, frightened almost to the breaking point.

The bandit, a strange smile upon his lips, and hidden laughter in his eyes, knew his power. The situation was one in which he reveled. He gazed around him, triumphantly. His legs were spread apart, a cigarette drooped nonchalantly from his lips.

"Senors, senoras!" he announced, in fascinating broken English, "you are all my preesoner!"

CHAPTER VIII

WHEREIN THE BANDIT EXPOUNDS A NEW PHILOSOPHY, AND MAKES MARIONETTES OF THE AMERICANS

"Put all ze men outside," Lopez ordered. Venustiano and Pedro, his chief lieutenants, obeyed at once, forcing them to march ahead of them, and standing guard over them near a great cactus bush a few feet from the adobe. "Leave ze women with me," the bandit continued. "But first, Alvarada, you find ze cook. I am 'ongry."

"*Si*," answered Alvarada; and after he had made certain that Pedro and Venustiano could handle the three men, one of whom, after all, was but an invalid in a wheel chair, he made his way to the kitchen. He knew there were two other companions who would help in any emergency. They slunk in the background, cigarettes between their lips, guns always ready for action. The house was completely surrounded.

Lucia and Angela, left alone with Lopez, revealed the deep concern they felt. They watched the bandit as he pawed through some papers on the table. With maddening indifference he then lighted another cigarette, and went over to the door, looking out at the male prisoners. Finally he turned upon them, looked them over, and remarked:

"What a pity. Only two women!"

They shuddered away from his gaze.

There was a noise from the direction of the kitchen, and Alvarada, with the miserable little Mexican cook ahead of him, rushed in.

He was addressing him in Spanish: "*Usted si cusinero. Borachi!*"

Lopez gave one glance at the poor specimen who had charge of the kitchen.

"The cook," he laughed. "He is dronk!" He now addressed him directly: "You are dronk," he affirmed, and stamped his foot.

Frightened, the boy cried: "No! No!" Certainly he was under the influence of the deadly tequila; but when he saw the bandit's face, and realized that he was in his power, he became suddenly and miraculously sober. He was firmly convinced that his last moment on this earth had come. He knew that a man like Lopez never hesitated to shoot to kill. He realized in the twinkling of an eye how late it was, how the dinner had been delayed through his drunkenness; and this visitor would brook no further waiting. He fully expected to be shot against the door. Therefore, to save time, he slunk to the entrance of the kitchen, placed himself against the jamb, crossed himself, muttered a rapid, incoherent prayer in Spanish, put his hands behind his back, closed his eyes and waited for the fatal shot that would send him straight to hell.

But nothing happened. Lopez looked at the cook, and said casually to Pedro:

"Not till after dinner," and puffed his cigarette.

"*Despues de la comida,*" said Pedro.

"I will make for you!" cried the wretched cook, opening his eyes, and so relieved to be still alive that he could scarcely articulate.

"*Pronto*," ordered Lopez.

"*Si, Madre di Dios!*" cried the cook; and fled to his kitchen, tumbling over himself in his eagerness to get a meal for the bandit.

There was a pause. What would Lopez do next? Kill them all? In Spanish he began, turning to Lucia:

"*Santa Maria* - You come here."

Angela stepped forward.

"You mean me?" she asked, sweetly.

"No!" came the gruff voice of Lopez. "You!" pointing to the frightened Lucia.

"Why do you want me?" she asked, moving slightly toward him.

"I would look at you," the bandit replied. He was appraising her already. "Turn around." She obeyed, like an automaton, "'Ow old are you?"

She would not lie. "Twenty-four," she answered.

"Ees pretty old," laughed Lopez. "Let me see your teeth."

"My teeth!" echoed Lucia. Did he take her for a horse?

Lopez merely nodded; and, with all the self-control she could bring to her aid, she opened her mouth and showed her wonderful teeth.

"*Si*," remarked Lopez, evidently pleased at the sight. "An' now, 'ow much weigh?"

"I don't know exactly," Lucia said.

"What's your name?" the bandit went on.

"Lucia." "Lucia!" he rolled the name over on his tongue, and smiled. "Lucia!" he repeated. "Ees nice name." Then, "Come 'ere. Come 'ere!" He did not wait for her to move this time. He put out his hand and drew her close to him. "I would see more of you," he told her. And, to her amazement and horror, he lifted her skirt delicately, almost tenderly. Her womanhood revolted at his action. This barbarian! She slapped his hand. But Lopez paid no more attention to the blow than if a child had struck him. "Not bad," he went on, indifferently, referring to her well-turned ankle. "'Ow you like to go wiz me to Mexico? Well?" when she did not answer. "You 'eard what I said."

That she should be insulted thus! "But - oh, I couldn't do that!" she cried out, in terror.

"Why not?" Lopez demanded.

"I'm - married."

"Well, we will not take ze 'usband! Just you an' me. We go to ze bull-fight. I rob ze jewelry store for you. We get plenty dronk." She shuddered. "Sure! I show you 'ell of a good time. Well, 'ow you say?" He glared at her, almost winked, smiled, and let a ring of smoke curl upward.

Lucia turned away, ashamed, mortified. "I never heard of such a thing!" she cried. Lopez laughed. "Deedn't nobody ever offer you good time before?" "Not like this." Lucia thought if he didn't stop soon, she would shriek.

"No? You 'ave been married all your life wiz one man?"

"Yes," she told him.

"My! what a rotten life you 'ave led!" the bandit commiserated her. "But ees not too late. I shall steel save you. But you shall not sank me. Shall not be so damn bad for me, too!"

Definite terror seized Lucia now. She knew by his tone, by his every gesture, that he was not fooling. She had heard, had read, of men like this Lopez. They were thick along the border. He meant business. Morgan had not exaggerated the danger of coming down here.

"But you wouldn't do that," she cried out.

"Why not?" Lopez said.

"It's - it's wrong!"

The bandit smiled his winning smile. "Whose beeziness what we do if we like for do him?"

"Please don't take me with you!" Lucia appealed. Why had Morgan Pell ever brought her to this border line? She might have known better than to come. It was no place for a young and attractive woman.

"You don't wish to go?" Lopez questioned, hardly believing that any pretty woman could resist his charms.

"No," cried Lucia.

"You mean you wish to stay married wiz one man?"

"Ye-es," Lucia faltered.

"Never no life? Never no fun? Ha! If you was old, fat - zen, perhaps. But young, beautiful! For why was you born if you no wish to leeve?"

"But I do wish to live!" Lucia cried in desperation; and her hands went out in an attitude of supplication.

Lopez appraised her once more. "But when I come along an'

show you 'ow you raise 'ell and say no. Ees great honor to be took by Pancho Lopez into Mexico. Like 'ow you say, ze decoration for ze chest," and he indicated the spot on his coat where a war medal might be placed.

Just then, to Lucia's relief, the cook came in, bearing a tray laden with chile con carne, bread and butter, and sugar, and placed it on the table. His fright was still evident. His hands trembled, his legs shook.

"Ah! Ze food!" Pancho cried. "Good! Put zem zere!" he ordered; and the cook placed the tray closer to him. Then he turned to Lucia Pell. "You shall wait on me," he told her, as though he were conferring the greatest honor upon her.

Angela came close to him, eager again to please him. He merely pushed her to one side, and had eyes only for Lucia. "You!" he said, looking her straight in the face. He sat down, and scanned the tray, while the cook stood in terror, not daring to leave the room, but wishing to God this moment were over. Had he forgotten anything?

"I do not see ze coffee," Pancho said at last.

"I get for you!" the cook screamed in a shrill voice, and rushed for the kitchen.

"*Pronto*," Lopez said. Then, to Lucia, "Ze bread." She leaned over to get a piece for him. He watched her carefully. "Your hand is shake. For why? You 'fraid from me, perhaps?"

She admitted that she was afraid - a little.

"And why?" he inquired.

"Because I've heard that you kill people," she bravely told him.

"Oh, but that isn't so!" Angela broke in, fearful that the mere mention of killing would bring about a murder then and there.

"I'm sure it isn't!" Nothing must be said to raise the thought in Pancho's mind.

"Why are you so sure?" Lopez demanded.

"It couldn't be! It couldn't be!" Angela declared. "Anyone so romantic as you, so -" And she tried to look her pleasantest. He must be placated, this wretched man.

"You are wrong," Lopez informed her, and also the entire room, "I do kill." Lucia, who had taken a seat near him, now drew back in alarm. He was quick to see her action.

"You need not be afraid," he heartened her. "I shall not 'urt you. That is, not yet. The chile -" she dished some out for him, hurriedly. "So! You are afraid of me because I kill people, eh?" He leaned back, and his lids contracted until his eyes looked wicked and sinister. The spangles on his sleeves trembled like leaves.

"A little," Lucia managed to say.

"You sink it wrong to kill?" Pancho wanted to know, gulping down a great mouthful of chile, and smattering a huge slice of bread with butter. He ate with his knife, like a glutton. He smacked his lips, and wiped them on the sleeve of his coat, where the brass buttons gleamed picturesquely.

"You talk of killing in such a matter-of-fact way," Lucia observed.

"An' why not?" Lopez asked.

The cook brought in the coffee-pot and put it on the table.

"Does life mean as little to you as that?" Lucia asked another question. This man was an enigma. He was bad through and through. They were as helpless as cattle in his hands.

Charles Hanson Towne

"Life?" Lopez smiled. "To be 'ere - zat is life. Not to be 'ere -" he gulped down some steaming coffee - "zat is death. Life is a leetle thing - unless it is one's own." He put the big cup down and put in four spoonfuls of sugar, stirred it diligently, and looked around him, the wonder of a child in his face.

"You do kill your prisoners, then?" Lucia brought out.

"Sure!" laughed Pancho.

Could she have heard aright? "You do?" she cried, and her cheeks took on an ashen hue.

"*Ciertamente!*" the bandit stated, as though they were talking of the weather. "You capture ze preesoner. You 'ave no jail to put 'im in. You pack him around wiz you. If you let 'im go, 'e come back to fight you again. So you kill him. Eet is very simple."

"But it seems so cold-blooded!" Lucia said.

"Ah! to you, perhaps! It is ze difference between zose who live in safety and zose who live in danger. In safety you 'ave ze bill to pay. You pay it and you forget it. In danger you 'ave enemy to kill. You kill 'im an' you forget 'im. *Save?*" And another heaping knifeful of the chile con carne went into his mouth.

"It's too horrible!" said Lucia; and she turned away.

"Ees life too horrible?" Pancho wanted to know.

"I never knew life was like that!" she said.

"Because you 'ave never really lived," the bandit explained. "Because you 'ave been always protect by ozzers. I kill only men. And only evil men. And when I kill evil man, it make me very 'appy. For I 'ave did a good deed." His simple philosophy pleased him.

"But who decides whether a man is good or evil'"

"I do!" answered Lopez, quick as a flash, and wondering how she could have asked so stupid a question.

"Oh, do let me pour some more coffee for you!" Angela begged.

"If you wish," Lopez said, indifferently. It mattered little to him now who waited upon him. His inner man had been partially satisfied. He leaned back in his chair, at peace with all the world. One spurred and booted foot was on the table.

"Oh, thank you!" Angela was all smiles. She was making headway with this evil man. "Thank you so much," she followed up, and, standing sweetly at his left, she poured the brown stuff into his cup. "Lovely weather, isn't it?" she remarked. The cook took the pot from her, and went back to the kitchen with it.

"*Si*," Lopez said. "Sit down. Sit down." Angela thought of course he was speaking to her, and being kind to her because of her girlish attentions. So she promptly seated herself. "No, not you!" Pancho said roughly, putting six spoons of sugar in this second cup. "You, I mean," indicating Lucia once more. Angela pouted, and turned her back on this bad, bad man. Pancho never even noticed her. The more opulent beauty of Lucia appealed to the sensuous in him. "You," he repeated. "Tell me, senora, 'ave you never been to a free country?"

Lucia was surprised at his question.

"A free country?" she said.

"Yes; like Mexico, for instance."

"Don't you call the United States a free country?" Lucia asked him.

Charles Hanson Towne

He almost roared his head off. "The United - Bah! Ees the most unfree country what is. Every man, every woman, is slave - slave to law, slave to custom, slave to everysing. You get up such time; eat such time," his hands went out in Latin frenzy. "Every day you work such time, every night go to bed such time. And, *Madre di Dios*, every week you take bath such time!" This was, to him, the ultimate joke. "An' you call it a free country! Ees only one free country. Ees one in which man does as she damn please. Like Mexico!" he ended.

The women were astounded. They had always thought of Mexico as a land of rough-and-tumble, comic-opera revolutions; a place where one must forever be on the lookout for trouble; where robbers were rife and the days were nothing but a chain of abominations. A sunny, beautiful country, maybe; but no place for a God-fearing American citizen to settle. Why, they would as soon commit murder in Mexico as go to market.

"Haven't you any laws in Mexico?" Lucia inquired.

"We 'ave - ze best," Lopez was swift to reply.

"But you just said -" Angela started to remind him, and took a little stool and moved close to him, seating herself upon it. She did not want him to forget her girlish sweetness. Lopez paid no heed to her.

"They are ze best because each man makes them for 'imself. Not like New York, where everybody tell you what you cannot do until zere is nozzing left what you want to do."

Angela piped up: "You've been to New York?"

"When I was agent for Madero - yes. I live at ze big hotel. I 'ave planty money. Ees no damn prohibition. I get dronk. I 'ave 'ell of a time. Sure! I see 'im all! New York!" he smiled in recollection.

"And you didn't like it?" Angela persisted, moving her little stool even closer to him.

"Like it? It makes me seeck! Even beautiful woman what I see 'ave 'osband what is afraid for 'er. Each time I get dronk comes big policeman which 'it me on ze 'ead." He smiled at the thought, "When I go to ze teatro, ees someone which 'ide under - ze bed. Not even can I step on ze grass because - New York! It crush ze 'eart!" He put both hands over his chest, and looked up at the ceiling.

"Yes!" exclaimed Angela, her stool very close to him now.

"Ees a prison for ze soul!" Lopez affirmed. "A stupid, seely place, your New York!"

"Yes!" Angela agreed again.

"For me New York can go to 'ell just as soon as she damn please!" the bandit let out.

"Oh, Mr. Robber!" Angela cried.

"But Mexico! How different!" Lopez said, paying no more attention to Angela than he would to a fly.

"I'm sure it is!" the girl said.

To Lucia, Lopez went on: "You shall see! Ze beautiful woman 'ave 'osband. But shall I not 'ave beautiful woman?"

"Oh, Mr. Bandit!" Angela put in once more.

"When we get dronk, ees not policeman which will 'it us on ze 'ead, but us which will 'it policeman on ze 'ead." Angela chuckled at this. "In ze teatro shall not be someone which 'ide under ze bed, but in it! You shall see! In Mexico ze heart leap! Ze soul she is free! You can do what you want - zat is, onless someone shoot you. Leesten, senora." He leaned close to

Lucia, who had not ventured to move, "Did you ever know the joy of fierce leeving? Did you?"

But she did not reply. Instead, it was the impetuous Angela who answered him:

"Yes. I mean, no!"

Lopez turned and scowled at her. "I was not spik to you," he said.

"You weren't!" Angela looked her surprise.

"*Ciertamente* no!" the bandit said.

Angela was hurt. "But you're not cross with me, are you?" she almost wept.

"No! I am not cross wiz you! Eez zat you annoy me!" And as though she were a doll, he pushed her from him, his big hand almost blotting out her pretty little face. The stool and Angela fell to the floor. She was furious. The devil in her was roused. Chagrined, she picked herself up. Her dainty plaid frock was covered with dust. She brushed it off as best she could, and cried:

"How dare you push my face, you bad man!"

"You should keep your face to home," Lopez answered, not turning a hair. He hadn't meant to be cruel. The incident was nothing to him. When anyone was in his way, he always got the obstacle out of it. He addressed the silent Lucia, who was horrified at the treatment accorded the innocent Angela. "Now that we have all finished eating," he said, delighting in the sarcasm, since no one else had had a bite, "we will get down to business." He shoved the tray aside, and the cook began instantly to clean things up. "Pedro!" Lopez called, taking out a huge ivory toothpick which he shamelessly used.

Instantly Pedro was at the door. "*Si!*" he said.

Lopez still spoke to Lucia: "We shall have big time togezzer - at least for a leetle while." Then he motioned to Pedro; and his men brought in the male prisoners. "You will not worry 'bout being married, once you come wiz me."

Morgan Pell heard this last remark.

"Look here," he said, "that's my wife you're talking to!" Rage was in his face. He didn't care whether he was this man's prisoner or not. There should be no insults hurled at Lucia - that old, primitive feeling for his woman was roused.

"So!" was all Lopez said, turning on Pell, and nodding his head. "Ees nice wife - I like her. You do not mind, do you?" His hand touched Lucia's arm. "Ees all right. I shall ask no question. You shall answer what I ask. And as is my custom, anybody what does not tell ze truth shall be quite suddenly -" he paused just the portion of a second - "shot."

Uncle Henry had rolled in with the rest. At this last word his chair reared up like a frightened steed. "Shot!" he cried.

"*Si*," answered Lopez, calmly.

"You mean it?" Uncle Henry asked, unbelief in his tone.

The bandit glared at him.

"Should I waste my time listening to sings which are not true?"

"Thank Gawd, I ain't got nothin' to lie about!" was Uncle Henry's relieved thought, expressed aloud.

"H'm!" Lopez murmured. "You have given me a idea." He rubbed his hands together, and then pushed his big sombrero a little back on his forehead. "Better as my own. I shall use it."

Uncle Henry wondered what he had suggested. "What's that?" he asked.

Lopez took on the voice of an orator, or a man in court making an important announcement. "If anyone 'ere shall tell me a lie, zen you shall all be -" he paused dramatically once more - "shot." The final word rang out like a shot itself.

A movement of despair ran through the group.

"Geemoneddy!" Uncle Henry broke the tension.

Lopez turned to Lucia. "All bot you," he graciously informed her. "I 'ave ozzer plans for you!" Her hair enraptured him - her youth and loveliness.

The relief she felt at the first part of the sentence was quickly killed as the sinister meaning of the latter part rushed into her brain.

"Other plans!" she cried.

"*Si.*" He was unmoved by her apprehension. He walked to the very center of the room, and looked about him, studying all their faces.

It was as if he were a central pivot and their destinies revolved around him. They had no idea what he would say next, and they hung on his words.

CHAPTER IX

WHEREIN UNCLE HENRY CHATTERS
SOME MORE, THERE IS AN AUCTION,
AND THINGS LOOK BLACK INDEED

"And now for business," Lopez said. "And remember zat he what tells a lie shall be right away shotted." In his excitement he lost the little English he had.

"I only hope *he* tells one!" Uncle Henry couldn't help saying, pointing to Hardy.

"You wish him to be shot?" the bandit wanted to know.

"Absolutely!" Uncle Henry was quick to answer.

Angela was horrified. "You want him to kill my dad?"

"I should enjoy it tremendous," Uncle Henry kept right on, and all but smacked his thin old lips.

Lopez was interested. "Why," he said slowly, wishing to get at the bottom of things, "do you wish him to be shotted so tremendous?"

Uncle Henry had no hesitation in answering: "Because he come to skin us out of this place, gol darn him!" And then, as if to save his skin, he pushed his chair far into the alcove, and, from this vantage point, watched to see what Hardy would do

Charles Hanson Towne

and say. He was aware that he had gotten him in a devilish stew. It served him right. He was a robber, a thief, and he didn't care what became of him. If Lopez took him out and had him shot at once he wouldn't have felt a qualm.

The bandit weighed what Smith had said; then he spoke directly to Hardy. "Zis is so? Zis is true?"

"No." The monosyllable was more emphatic than any long explanation could have been. A scowl on his brow, Hardy came close to Lopez, fearlessly. "I came to foreclose a mortgage I hold on this place. That is all."

But Uncle Henry was not going to see him get away with that. "Tell him why you want this ranch so bad!" he yelled. "I dare you!"

Pell now stepped forward. Their predicament was bad enough as it was, without having this old imbecile make it worse. "Keep still, you fool! Do you want to get us into more trouble?"

"I certainly do," cried Uncle Henry, "an', gol darn it, I'm a-goin' to! Rob me of ten thousand dollars, will you?"

Lopez was listening with both ears; and a glint came into his eyes, "Zat is true?" he inquired, interested anew. "He has rob you of ten sousand dollars? Eh - heh - a good beeg sum!"

"Ask him!" Uncle Henry said. "An' I only hope to thunder he tells a lie!" His voice went up on a high key.

The bandit looked keenly at Morgan Pell. "Did you?" There was no reply. "You hear me - you will answer - at once!"

"No." Morgan Pell shot out the word, and clenched his fists. The situation was becoming hot. This old fellow would have them all dead in a few moments if he didn't keep his mouth shut.

A look of triumph came into Uncle Henry's eyes. "There's your big chance!" he shouted to Lopez. "Shoot him quick!"

But Pell said calmly: "I paid twenty thousand dollars for an option on the place."

"Yes, but you didn't give me the money!" Uncle Henry insisted.

"I was going to," the other replied, not even casting a glance over his shoulder.

Old man Smith turned to Lopez. "Oh! You didn't shoot quick enough! I got it now! Ask him why he wants the place! Maybe he'll tell another one!" And he tittered with glee.

Lopez put the question to Pell.

"I - I -" the latter stammered; but could get no farther.

Uncle Henry was gleeful now. "Get ready!" he yelled to Lopez. "He's going to do it! Keep your hand on your gun!"

"I thought," Pell brought out reluctantly, "I thought there might be - oil on it."

Lopez was dumbfounded. This was far more interesting than even he had calculated.

"Oil?" he said.

Pell looked down. "But I think, under the circumstances, I shall not take up my option." The paper was in his hand, and Lopez, seeing it, reached as if to take it, when Pell handed the document to him. "In which case," Pell informed the bandit, "the place would belong to him," shrugging a shoulder toward Uncle Henry.

"What's that?" the latter asked.

"- making him a very rich man indeed," Pell added, significantly.

Aghast at the turn affairs had taken, Uncle Henry could scarcely speak. "Well, for the love o' Mike!" he managed to say.

The bandit now turned full upon Uncle Henry, who was still concealed in the shadow of the alcove. "Ah! so you would have all ze money!"

"No, I wouldn't!" Uncle Henry protested. "I -" He quickly put his hand to his mouth, stopping it like a child caught in a lie. "I mean - yes, I wouldn't! Only we ain't found the oil yet. And personally, I don't believe there's any here in the first place!" Realizing what he had said, he caught himself again. "I mean, it may be here, but - Don't shoot yet! I'll get it in a minute!" he begged. He was agitated to the breaking point.

Hardy stepped forward, "Wait. I've a suggestion to offer," he said.

"Yes?" Lopez uttered the word as though he had grave doubts.

"You're after money," the tall, lank neighbor said. "I'll tell you how we can make some - make a lot."

"Well?" said Lopez, still far from convinced, and taking things easily.

Hardy spoke more rapidly. "If the mortgage I hold on this property isn't paid by eight o'clock to-night, it becomes mine. Keep that paper here until eight o'clock, and I'll give you ten thousand dollars!" He watched the effect of his words on the Mexican.

Pell spoke before the bandit. "Why, damn you -" he began, to Hardy.

But the latter paid no attention to his insult. He faced Lopez, as though he were the only person in the room. "What do you say, is it a go?"

"Wait a minute!" Pell cried.

Lopez faced him. "Yes?" And puffed his cigarette.

Pell addressed both the bandit and Jasper Hardy. "I'll make a better offer. Keep *him* here until eight o'clock, and I'll give you twenty thousand dollars!"

Lopez was considering, "H'm," he murmured, and stroked his chin.

Uncle Henry saw a mess ahead. He steered right into the group, crying, "Wait a minute. I got a better idea yet!"

"You?" Lopez said, as he might have addressed a moron.

"Yes, this place don't belong to neither of 'em yet!"

"But who does it belong to?" the Mexican wanted to know.

"My nevyer," the invalid said.

"And which is 'e?"

"He's down in the shed - fixin'," the old man informed him.

Lopez turned to Pedro. "Venustiano shall find him. Before he make trouble - you," turning to "Red," "shall show 'im where." Pedro had raised his revolver; and one look at it was enough for "Red." These bandits meant what they said; more, they meant every gesture they made.

"It's all right," the foreman said. "He ain't got anything to lose anyhow. I'll show you where he is," and, followed by the sinister Venustiano, he went out.

Uncle Henry moved his chair close to Lopez. "Now listen, robber - I mean, bandit. You keep both these fellers here and lend us ten thousand dollars, and we'll give you a million!"

"A million!" said Lopez, his eyes big.

"The first million we make out of the oil that's here!" "Uncle Henry proposed. And, serious as things were getting to be, a smile went around the group.

"I should lend you ten sousand dollar?" the bandit asked.

"Absolutely! Will you?" Uncle Henry had the temerity to say.

"I do not lend," was the hard response. "I take." And he turned away.

"But if you'll -" the old man pleaded.

"Your proposition not interests me," Lopez said. Uncle Henry wheeled over to the staircase. The bandit turned to Pell. "You offer me twenty sousand? Zat is so?" he said.

"Right," Pell replied.

Lopez smiled sardonically, "Twenty sousand - for what is worth millions?"

"But I don't know that there's oil here," Pell argued.

Lopez laughed. "No?" Then, to Hardy, "You? You don't know, eizer, I s'pose?"

"I thought there might be - that's all."

The bandit gave a hearty laugh. "Oh!" he exclaimed, almost consumed with mirth. "I see I do business wiz business men - wise business men. *Bueno*! Now we three business men togezzer, eh? Suppose I shall show you where ze oil is. What zen?" He looked around the room, as if he thought everybody should be interested; and indeed everyone was. Little gasps came from Hardy and Pell, and Uncle Henry wiggled his chair up closer.

"Show us where she is?" Hardy asked, breathless.

"*Si*," Lopez answered.

"There *is* oil here?" Pell asked excitedly.

Another cigarette went into the bandit's mouth. "Should I waste time talking of what ain't?" he drily said.

Hardy was still skeptical. "You know there's oil on this ranch?"

"I 'ave know so for a long time."

"On the level?" said Pell, eagerly.

"'Way down below," laughed Lopez, delighted at his ability to pun in English, and making a motion with one hand toward the nether regions.

"You mean it?" Pell continued.

A dark scowl came over the face of Lopez. "Should you doubt my word?" he inquired.

"Certainly not," Pell was quick to satisfy him. "Only why didn't you say so before?"

"Oil not interests me," the bandit explained.

"But since to you gentlemen it seem so excitable - I 'ave it."

"Yes?" from Hardy.

"Ze little paper. You both want it. *Bueno!* You shall both 'ave ze chance. We will, 'ow you say, 'old ze little hauction."

"Auction?" Pell repeated.

"'E who bids ze 'ighest," Lopez elucidated, "shall 'ave ze little paper and shall come wiz me while I show 'im where ze oil she is 'iding." He flicked the ashes of his cigarette upon the floor, and sat on the corner of the table, one foot dangling in the air.

"Gad!" Pell let out. His hands went together, his jaw set. Things were coming out beautifully.

Lopez went on: "While 'e who does not bid ze 'ighest shall stay 'ere wiz Pedro until eight o'clock to-night."

Hardy was delighted. "You mean the highest bidder will not only get the place but that you'll show him where the oil is besides?"

"*Si.* Is it so agree?"

"I'm for that," Pell said.

"But I -" Hardy began.

"I bid one hundred thousand dollars," Pell quickly cried.

"I'll take it to the courts," Hardy contended.

"Take what to the courts?" Pell wanted to know.

"I was detained by force," Hardy said.

"As long as I get there by eight, what difference does that make?" Pell asked.

But Lopez broke in: "One hundred sousand I am offer!" They mustn't shillyshally this way. He wanted to keep things going.

"I'll make it one hundred and one!" Hardy cried.

Without a moment's hesitation, Pell jerked it up to a hundred and ten.

"A hundred and eleven!" Hardy pushed ahead.

"A hundred and twenty-five!" Pell yelled. "And what do you know about that?"

Hardy was by no means finished. "A hundred and thirty!" he made it.

Uncle Henry couldn't stand it. While they raised each other's bids, he shot in between them and managed to say above the din, "And me - gettin' skinned not only out of my ten thousand, but a million dollars besides!"

"A hundred and fifty!" Pell was saying.

"A hundred and fifty-one!" the cautious Hardy added.

The face of Lopez was a study; but they were so excited that they did not look at him. Angela rushed to her father and clasped his arm when she heard his last raise. "That's right, father. Don't let him get it!"

"Don't worry," he reassured her, and patted her little hand, so warm on his arm. He turned to Pell. "You city fellers needn't think you can come down here and put it all over us."

"Nevertheless," said Morgan Pell, "I'll just bid a hundred and seventy-five thousand."

"Then I'll make it a hundred and eighty!" his antagonist stated.

Quick as a flash, "A hundred and ninety," Pell said.

"Two hundred, by darn!" yelled Hardy, furious now.

"Two hundred and -" Pell began; when Lopez, to their amazement, rapped on the table with his gun, as though he were an auctioneer and this his gavel, "Senors!" he shouted. "It is enough!"

Everyone was dumbfounded, "Enough?" Hardy inquired, unbelieving.

"Too much!" Lopez explained.

"What's the idea?" Pell, shrewder than before, wanted to know. His brow contracted. So there was a fly in the ointment, after all!

"Ze idea, my friend, is zis," Lopez calmly stated. "I am not interest in pieces of paper. I do not accep' checks. Also I am no damn fool! You sink I sink you bring back two 'ondred sousand dollar? Two 'ondred sousand soldier, mebbe! But two 'ondred sousand dollar! Pah!" and he made a gesture of disgust, and crushed the paper in his hand and let it fall on the floor under the table.

"Then what's the idea of this auction in the first place?" Pell asked, mad through and through that they had been tricked by this Mexican fool.

Lopez leaned back on the table. "To find out if you gentlemen was rich enough to make it worth my w'ile to take you wiz me and 'old you for ransom." His eyes half closed. He was enjoying their discomfiture. There was nothing he liked more than to spring a surprise like this.

Pell and Hardy looked at each other, real terror in their faces now.

"Ransom!" the former cried.

"It is quite to be seen zat you are," the bandit grinned. "Zis, if I may speak so, 'as been a lucky day for me!"

Pell turned to both Hardy and Lopez, and addressed them: "Bluffing, were you?"

Lopez was quick to retort: "And was you bluffing when you bidded ze two 'ondred sousand dollars?"

Hardy was agitated. "I'm afraid we were a bit hasty," he tried to explain things away.

This tickled Uncle Henry's bump of humor. He chuckled, and cried, "Ho, ho! Serves you both gol darn good and right!" He seemed to go into a spasm of laughter.

Pell's chief concern now was to get out of the mess - to get away; to have everything settled. Lopez could probably be dealt with, man to man.

"Look here," he suggested, in a direct attack, "can't we settle things some way?"

"Yes," the bandit replied. "From my headquarters in Chihuahua I will give you pen, ink, messenger-boy - everysing!"

"But I -" Pell started to say.

But Lopez broke in: "You will please listen more and speak less. I 'ave decide. You I shall 'old for ransom. And," turning to Hardy, "you; and you," pointing to Uncle Henry, "you who 'ave nossing, I shall leave be'ind."

Pell and Hardy felt that the game was over.

Uncle Henry, on the contrary, was jubilant. "Gee!" he sang out, "and I get the oil, after all!"

No one heeded him. Things were too serious still.

"You wouldn't do this?" Hardy asked of Lopez.

Charles Hanson Towne

"No?" the bandit asked.

Hardy took Angela in his arms. "But what about her - my daughter? You wouldn't take her, would you?"

"Not for a million dollars!" Lopez smiled.

Angela's pride was hurt, "H'm!" she sniffed.

Lopez looked around him. He saw Lucia, and extended his hand to her. "And as for you -" he began.

Lucia was frightened. What was to be her fate?

"Yes?" she breathed.

"Life 'as been unkind to you. Too long 'ave you been marry wiz ze tired business man. You shall come wiz me to ze land of purple mountains, where I will love you myself personal."

This animal! Lucia turned from him in horror. "But I don't want to love!"

"It is not what you want," a new tone came into Lopez's voice. "It is what *I* want. I am ze law, 'ere!"

"Please!" Lucia pleaded.

Pell stepped forward. "Look here!" he cried. "There must be some way out of this!"

"Zere is," said Lopez politely. He pointed to the door. "Zat way."

Angela clung to her father's neck. "Dad!" she cried, seeing that he was about to be forced to go - perhaps forever. Tears rolled down her pretty cheeks.

Pell saw the seriousness of things now, and turned to Hardy in a strange camaraderie. "I guess we're up against it," he said.

"Looks that way," the other replied. In their misfortune they were curiously united.

Lopez turned to the whole room. "If you are ready?" he said, and snapped his fingers as a slave-driver might have done. "Pedro!" he called, "kill ze first one what make trouble," indicating the entire group of prisoners. Pedro grinned hopefully. "Zey go. *Bueno!* Zey go - all of zose ozzers. I shall follow - wiz my woman." He turned to Lucia, who was standing like a graven image near the table. "Come! We shall be very 'appy togezzer, you and me!"

They were about to pass through the door - all of them - when a noise startled them; and Gilbert, followed by "Red" and Venustiano, appeared.

CHAPTER X

WHEREIN AN OLD FRIENDSHIP COMES TO LIFE, LOPEZ LEARNS A THING OR TWO, AND FINALLY MAKES A MATCH

"What's coming off?" Gilbert said, looking about him, and not a little surprised to find a Mexican and his adherents in his adobe.

Lopez turned and gave him a searching look. A light seemed to come into the bandit's countenance. It was as if someone had put a lantern behind his face.

"You!" he cried, enraptured. "You ze nephew zat owns zis ranch?"

Gilbert came farther into the room. Everyone now had turned back, stood stock still, listening to these two.

"Yes," said young Jones. "I am. What of it?" He didn't understand matters at all. Absent from the house for a little time, he had been called back to find this medley of people.

Lopez searched his face again. "Tell me you 'ave been in Canon Diabalo sometime? 'Ave you?"

"Of course. What of it?" Gilbert was mystified.

"You were there one night, three, mebbe four year ago?" Lopez persisted, hoping there could be no mistake.

"I don't remember," was the disappointing answer.

"You remember poor peon was wounded - near bleed to death?"

"What?" said Gilbert, light beginning to dawn upon him.

"You do!" shouted Lopez, delighted. "Where was 'e wounded? Quick! You tell!"

"Shot through the shoulder," Gilbert answered promptly.

"It is you! Don't you know me?" He faced him squarely, threw back his shoulders, and waited, breathless, for his look of recognition.

Gilbert studied his face. An instant of doubt, and then, "Why, you're Pancho Lopez!" he said.

The bandit was overjoyed. "I am! But don't you recognize who is ze Pancho Lopez what I am? Look close! Ze clothes, no! Ze face!"

"Good Lord!" was all Gilbert could utter.

"Now you know me?"

"You're the man I found wounded that night!"

"And whose life you save!" Lopez added.

"Well, what do you know about that!" young Jones shouted. He was as surprised and happy as the bandit himself. This man, whom he never thought to see again in his whole life was standing here, in his own adobe.

"Now you know me!" Pancho went on. "Ah! my frand! 'Ow

glad I am for to see you some more! Pedro! Venustiano! Ees my friend! Sabbe! Orders like my own! Serve 'im as you would me!" He went to Gilbert and frankly embraced him in the Latin fashion. "Eet's 'ell of a good thing I reckernize you!" he laughed, hugging his old friend close. He could never forget his kindness that night so many years ago; and to think he had run across his deliverer now!

Everyone was relieved. Their troubles would now be ended.

"And you ain't going to rob him, after all?" Uncle Henry piped up.

"Rob 'im? Rob my frand?" Lopez repeated.

"Ain't you?" Uncle Henry cried.

The bandit looked at him, wonder in his eyes. "No! *Ciertamente* no!"

"Hooray!" the old man yelled, and would have risen in his chair could he have done so.

"Say, who the 'ell is that?" said Lopez, addressing himself to Gilbert.

"He's my uncle," young Jones answered.

"Uncle?" the bandit said, unbelieving.

"Uncle Henry," old man Smith wanted it to be straight.

"He shall go free," Lopez announced.

Hardy thought this a good omen. They would all be set free, no doubt. He faced Lopez bravely. "Ah, then it's all right," he said, a sickly smile on his face.

"All right?" said Lopez.

"Yes," Hardy said.

Lopez considered for a moment, hand on chin, his eyes again two narrow slits. "Not so fast," he cautioned. "It ees all right for 'im," nodding at Uncle Henry, "an' all right for 'im," indicating Gilbert; "but for you -" He let one hand fly out, and a resounding slap on Hardy's eager face was the result. Then he turned to Pedro. "Take them all out - *pronto*! 'Ees all right!' Like 'ell ees all right!"

Hardy flushed scarlet. His first impulse was to strike back; but how could he? Those guns pointed at him from every direction. He was as powerless as a baby. But his hour would come. This dastardly Mexican bandit should suffer for that blow.

Yet like one of a line of sheep he was obliged to follow Pedro out of the door. It was a humiliating moment. Gilbert and Lopez were left alone.

"Now we shall visit," the bandit said, and put his arm through Gilbert's. "Ah! it ees so good to see you, my frand!"

Gilbert was still mystified. "Yes," he said, "but I don't understand how you, a peon, became the Pancho Lopez so soon."

"Ah! it ees so easy!" laughed the bandit.

"Easy!" Gilbert repeated.

"*Si*. My frand" - his hand went to Gilbert's shoulder - "ees great opportunity, ees revolution, for make speed. When I got well, I find I do not enjoy my work, which are 'ard. Business? Business, she make me sick! I say for myself, 'What to do?' Zen, suddenly I sink, 'I shall be soldado!' Soldier which shall be giv ze 'orse, ze gun, ze woman, and nozzing to do but shoot a little sometimes! Ees a wonderful life, my frand!" The smoke of his cigarette curled to the ceiling.

Charles Hanson Towne

"I didn't find it so," young Jones said, and smiled in his dry way.

"Pah! It's too many damn rules in your army. For us who make revolution, no! We sleep so late we damn please. We fight some when we feel so. If we find ze hacienda, we take all what we choose. When we need money, we go to city and rob ze bank - we 'elp for ourselves food from ze store, shoes, clothes, candy, ze cigarette, agauriante -" he made as if to drink from an imaginary glass - "booze! An' if anybody 'ide anysing we cut 'is fingers off so's 'e tell us. She is one fine life! You like for try? I make you general! Come!"

His face was radiant. The recollection of his army life filled him with joy.

But Gilbert shook his head. "Not for me, thank you," he smiled.

Lopez merely shrugged his shoulders. "So! I was afraid!"

"But how did you get ahead so fast?" young Jones wanted to know. "That's what sticks me."

The bandit laughed. "Zat is simple. You see, one day ze lieutenant she are killed. Soon I become a lieutenant. Nex' day, ze captain. So I am captain, Byme-bye, ze major - so I became major. Pretty damn soon ze colonel - so I am colonel. I kill ze general for myself." As he spoke, he lifted the chair at the table, and brought it down on the floor with a bang.

"What!" cried Gilbert, at this description of an opera-bouffe army.

"But we shall not talk of me," Lopez said. "We shall spik of you. 'Ow you been since I seen you, what?" He tossed away his cigarette.

Gilbert offered him another of his own.

"No, gratias; zat's for peon. Zese from ze swell hotel National an Torreon - zay are good. I steal zem myself," pulling out his case and lighting another. He pushed his chair so that he could see young Jones better. "Well, old frand, how you feel zis long time? Eh?"

"I?" said Gilbert. He smiled a little, and looked significantly about the room.

Lopez caught the look. "So?" he said, sympathy in his tone. "It ees too bad." He paused, letting the smoke curl over his head again. "Ah! I see her now! You are ze nephew of Uncle Henry which owns zis rancho which are to be foreclosed by moggidge." Gilbert nodded. "H'm! Zat shall make her all different some more! Axplain for me, so I shall know."

Gilbert replied: "There's not much to tell. I borrowed ten thousand from my uncle; ten more from Hardy - the tall man, and our neighbor. He's a loan shark - you know, in a mortgage. I go to the war. When I come home, cattle all gone. No money. That's all." He made a gesture as though the world were tumbling about him.

"I see," said Lopez. "And wiz ze strange ideas of your country, it makes you feel bad."

"Well, it seems like a pretty good chunk of trouble to hand an average citizen," young Jones said.

"Trouble?" Lopez let out the word in wrath. "You are no trouble. You only sink you are."

"You don't call this trouble? If it isn't then I don't know what trouble is!"

"Not really trouble." He came over and put his hand on Gilbert's shoulder. "Only trouble you are made for yourself because you go by law what are foolish instead of sense what are wise." He gave him an affectionate pat. Just then Uncle

Henry wheeled himself in, neither inquiring nor caring if he was wanted or not.

"Well, I sure told 'em their right names for once, gol darn 'em!" he chuckled. Lopez glared at him. "Pardon me! My mistake!" the invalid apologized; and rolled into the alcove. "So, you sink you have much trouble," Lopez continued, as though the invalid had not come in to interrupt them. The clock struck five. He listened to it, and then said, "I have time to spare -" He went to the window and looked out.

"But if you've been raiding around here," Uncle Henry said from his seclusion, "won't the rangers be after you?"

"I have ze scouts who watch," the bandit said. He turned to Gilbert again. "Suppose I stop here and prove to you who sink you have trouble, zat really you have no trouble at all?"

The young man looked at him incredulously. "You mean you can get me out of this mess?" he asked.

"Sure! In one half hour," the bandit was convinced.

"Really?"

"In one half hour your trouble go poof!" He made a ring of smoke and watched it fade away. "And you shall be 'appy man. If I do zat, what zen?"

"If you do that," said the other, "they'll have to tie me down to keep me from kissing you!"

"Good!" laughed Lopez. "She is did."

There was a moment's pause. Then, "But how are you going to do this miracle?" Gilbert was anxious to find out.

"Zat is for you to leave to me. Well, what you say?"

"I say yes, of course!"

"*Bueno!* We begin," said the bandit. He called through the door: "Pedro! Bring zem all in again."

Uncle Henry was curious, "What are you going to do?"

"You shall see," was all Lopez answered.

Angela was the first to file into the room. Uncle Henry glanced at her. "What are you going to do about her?" he asked.

Lopez looked around, "Her?" he said.

"Her!" repeated Uncle Henry.

"What 'as her to do wiz it?" the bandit inquired.

"Why, she wants to marry him," Uncle Henry revealed, pointing to his nephew. "That's what started the whole jamboree."

Lopez looked astonished. "So?" he said.

"Uh - huh!"

The bandit glanced at Gilbert. "But 'e does not love 'er," he said, nodding toward Angela.

"Certainly not!" Gilbert was instantly saying, and glared at his uncle. The latter, as usual, plunged straight ahead, as the others now gathered about the room. "He," meaning "Red," "loves her. *He*," he nodded toward his nephew, "loves *her*," pointing to Lucia Pell. "And she loves him," nodding back to Gilbert.

"Shut up! How many times must I tell you to -"

"But she," went on Uncle Henry, just as if nothing had been

said, and pointing to Lucia, "is married to him," indicating Pell. "Which makes it a hell of a mess all around!" He leaned back in his chair as if he had done a good day's work.

Gilbert could scarcely restrain himself. Again he wanted to lay violent hands upon him - he wished he could. "Be quiet, won't you?" he breathed.

"Not me!" Uncle Henry persisted. "I've gotter tell the truth."

"Yes, but - " Gilbert began.

"I don't wanter get shot," the old man declared.

Lopez turned to Gilbert. "Is it true? You love her?" his eyes going to Lucia.

How could he tell the truth? "Of course I do not," he affirmed. Then he went close to his uncle. "What did you do all this again for?"

"He says he can fix it," Uncle Henry said. "Let him try. He's done swell so far. Personally, I got a lot o' confidence in that feller. He's slick, he is!"

It was easy to be seen that the bandit was not satisfied with the answer Gilbert had given him. He had been slyly watching both him and Lucia. Now, he said, looking at them both: "So!" And old man Smith started to break in once more; but Lopez went on: "Is it true?"

"What makes you think so?" Gilbert wanted to know.

"It is in her eyes - and yours," the Mexican stated. "I shall miss her. She is very beautiful. However, what is one woman between frands?" He laughed a bitter laugh. "You shall have her."

Uncle Henry cried out: "But he can't have her. She's married."

"Ees too bad," said Lopez, nonchalantly. "But nozzing to get excite about."

"Nozzing to get excite about!" mimicked Uncle Henry.

"No. But ees more to be did zan I 'ave sought. But I 'ave promise I shall make you a 'appy man, my frand," again to Gilbert. "*Bueno!* I keep zat promise. You have gave me your word zat you will not interfere. Is it not so?"

"Yes, but I - " Gilbert hardly knew what to say.

"It is for you to keep zat word as I keep mine," Lopez said. Then, to Uncle Henry he went on, "I shall start wiz you. Now, Pedro!"

"*Si*," answered the faithful minion of the bandit, stepping forward.

"Remember," his master commanded. "Shoot ze first one which interrup'."

"*Si*," said Pedro again, and grinned broadly and pleasantly. If there was one thing he liked, it was the possibility of trouble with prisoners. He knew how to bring them to terms. He had been doing it for years.

Lopez got down to business. "Now, look here, Oncle Hennery: my frand 'ave borrow money which 'e 'ave lost? Is zat true?"

"Yes, sir," answered Uncle Henry promptly, and happy to have been addressed so familiarly by the bandit. He felt that his triumph was now complete.

"'E cannot be happy until 'e pay you back."

"No, sir," sitting up straight in his chair.

"I shall give you ten sousand dollar," was the bandit's

Charles Hanson Towne

surprising remark.

Uncle Henry thought he could not have heard aright. "Ten thousand -! Yes, but where are you going to get it?" he inquired, a bit dazed.

"Do not ask me." He caught sight of "Red." "Ze next is you." He appraised him rapidly, and then said to Gilbert, "'E is frand for you, no?"

"He certainly is," answered young Jones promptly. "About the best I ever had." He wasn't going to see anything happen to the faithful "Red." He'd have protected him with his own life.

Lopez liked this, "You love zat girl?" he said to the foreman, meaning, of course, Angela.

"What?" the latter cried out.

"Well, I don't go around advertising the fact," "Red" told Lopez, a bit mortified that his heart affairs should be thus openly discussed.

"Ze girl zat spoiled my dinner," the bandit laughed.

"Oh!" cried Angela, who thought she had done so well.

"And she love you?" Lopez went on.

"I don't either!" Angela protested, speaking before "Red" had a chance.

"Now, Angela!" said "Red," his face the color of his flaming hair.

His dream seemed so close. Was it possible that the only girl he ever had adored was going to see it wrecked?

Angela weakened a bit at his tone. "I like him," she told the bandit. "But I don't - love him."

"Ah! but you do!" Lopez insisted.

"I do?" said Angela, wide-eyed.

"I have so decide!" the bandit stated.

"What?" cried Angela, not knowing what he could be driving at.

"Also you make love to my frand, Senor Jones."

"Oh!" cried the frightened girl now.

"And you have annoyed him in other ways."

"I have?" she wailed, terrified to the breaking point.

"Red" intervened. "Listen, Angela -" he began.

She stamped her little foot, and was peppery at once. "I won't!"

"You don't love him," "Red" affirmed, for her.

"Oh!" Angela burst out, all confusion.

"No more than you loved any of the rest of 'em," "Red" went on.

"Keep still!" the girl cried. "Keep still! I think you're dreadful!"

"It's because they're better looking than me," her slave went right on. "I'm the one for you to marry, Angy, and you know it!" He had faith in himself at last - she couldn't stop him now.

"No!" Angela contradicted.

"Aw, come on!" poor "Red" begged.

But she stamped her foot again. "No - no - *no*!"

"Say you will!" "Red" pleaded, almost distracted.

But Angela was adamant. "I won't - I won't listen to you another minute!" She turned her back on him, blushing to the roots of her hair.

Lopez had been highly amused at the girl's pique and "Red's" honest interest in her. He came to his assistance. "We shall be patient. She is mad. And mad lady sink not wiz ze 'ead, but only wiz ze tongue." He faced the pouting Angela. "Senorita, leesten to me. 'Ow old are you?"

"None of your business!" was the instant answer.

"Twenty-eight? Twenty-nine?" Lopez pressed, smiling.

"Certainly not! I'm only twenty!" She was swift with the denial.

"Ah! I sought so," said Lopez, much pleased.

"What?" Angela said, not understanding him.

"In Mexico you would now be married five years -" the bandit explained.

"What?" screamed Angela.

"An' have six children."

"Oh!" The very thought made Angela ill.

"You are not pretty - none too pretty!" Lopez said.

The girl was now both hurt and amazed. "What's that?" she

cried, all her feminine anger aroused.

"You will soon grow fat," Lopez continued, looking her over carefully.

Angela pulled out her handkerchief and brushed her eyes. "Oh!"

"Like ze tub!" said Lopez, inexorably, spreading his arms to indicate an immense diameter.

"Oh!" was all poor Angela could get out.

"Also, you 'ave ze bad temper."

"Oh! Oh!" Sobs now came from her.

"So, if you do not marry soon, it will be too late."

"What's that?" she looked up, not able to believe she had understood.

"Now, my frand 'ere, 'e wish to marry wiz you. Why, I do not know." Lopez grinned broadly. He knew this would be the last stroke. He was right.

"Oh!" gasped Angela.

"Shall he come wiz me to Mexico," the bandit piled it on, "I will give 'im planty wives, young, beautiful...."

"Oh!" again came from the distracted Angela.

"But he want you. And so..."

"You're going to force me to marry him. I see!" She turned to the listening "Red." "And you'd let him force you on me, like this?"

Charles Hanson Towne

"It ain't my fault, Angela," the foreman assured her. "I didn't know he was going to do this! You know that."

Lopez issued his ultimatum.

"I am not going to force you to marry 'im. You are going to choose to marry 'im."

The girl was on the brink of despair.

"Never! Never! Never!" she screamed, and stamped her foot vigorously.

"Ah! my young lady. We shall see." He turned abruptly, and called, "Pedro!"

"*Si*," the faithful one answered, and came to his master.

Lopez then addressed Angela: "I shall not force you to marry 'im," indicating "Red" with a wave of the hand. "I shall insist only zat if you do not marry wiz 'im, you shall marry wiz Pedro."

Directly behind the girl stood the fearful Pedro. His face was the dirtiest that had ever crossed the border into Arizona. His teeth were sparse, his hair a tangled mass of grit and dirt; his hands like violent mud-pies. The suit he wore was stained and greasy - he had slept in it for many nights. Altogether, he was about the most hopeless-looking individual a girl could be asked to look upon. At his master's words, he grinned a fiendishly happy grin, spread out his arms as if to embrace the charming Angela, and, if possible, press a kiss upon her rosy cheek. But Angela, with one look at him, collapsed into "Red's" waiting arms. He seemed like heaven to her now.

"Ah!" yelled Lopez.

"'Red'! save me, save me!" Angela cried in melodramatic fashion.

Pedro, seeing how far from popular he was with the young lady, walked disconsolately to the door.

"So! You do love 'im, after all!" the bandit said to Angela.

"I never thought I could love anybody so much!" the girl replied. "Oh, 'Red'!" And she hugged him again.

"You mean it?" asked the delighted "Red." "You're not saying it because..."

But Lopez broke in: "She is saying it because it is ze truth. In pleasure, a woman go to ze man she sink she love. In fear, she go to ze man she really love....Well, you really want her? She is yours. And I 'ope you will be 'appy. At least, I 'ave done my part." He smiled his most enchanting smile.

"You have - you certainly have, and I am mighty obliged to you," said the grateful "Red."

"You are welcome. I like you. But remember zis: Eet is your wish - not mine....Don't blame me."

"Red" could stand this now: he had his Angela. And tucked in his big arm, he took her outdoors.

As soon as they had gone, Hardy turned to Lopez. "Look here!" he shouted, "I guess I've got something to say about this. That's my daughter, whose affairs you've been so kindly fixing up, and -"

Lopez gave him one look that closed his mouth suddenly. "Don't shoot, Pedro," he said. "Well?"

Hardy cast one eye at Pedro's lifted gun, and got out only one word, "Nothing." A meeker man never lived.

"From what my frand tell me, I can see now 'ow you make your money," the bandit told Hardy. "You are a robber."

Charles Hanson Towne

This was too much for Hardy - for any man with a spark of manhood left in him.

"I am not!" he denied. "I'm a business man."

"You are a loan fish," the bandit pressed.

"A what?"

"A loan fish! You loan money. And when ze people cannot pay, you convict zem and take zeir ranchos."

The lean, sharklike Hardy looked a little depressed at this accusation.

"Well, if they can't pay, it isn't my fault," was all he could say.

"It isn't zeir fault, too, is it?" Lopez was curious to know.

"What's that?" Hardy said.

"So you take ze rancho from my friend, Senor Jones. A nice sort of neighbor you are, you beeg fish!"

"I'm not to blame because he's a rotten business man, am I?" Hardy tried to set himself right.

Lopez looked at him scornfully. "How do you know 'e is a rotten business man?"

"Why, the fact that I've had to foreclose the mortgage shows that," Hardy smiled.

"Not at all. Senor Jones 'ave been away to war. He been away fighting for 'is country."

"Well, that isn't my fault."

"No." There was profound contempt in the little word. "He

give up 'is business to go away to fight to save you, while you stay be'ind to rob 'im. Is zat fair?"

Hardy gave a gesture of disdain. "I'm not talking about what's fair, or what's not fair. There's lots of things in this world that ain't right. I am doing only what the law allows." He thought this cleared his skirts. It was the refuge of every scoundrel.

"I do not speak about ze law," Lopez followed him up. "I am doing only what is fair. If I were you, I should be ashamed for myself! You love your country?"

"Certainly I do," the other answered.

"Like 'ell! You love yourself!" And Lopez deliberately turned his back on him.

"Now, wait a minute!" Hardy begged. He could scarcely have this insult added to the host of others. "I do love my country. I'm a good American."

"Yet you would rob ze man who fight for your country! Bah!" The bandit waved his hand in disgust.

Hardy saw he was in a bad hole. "There's some truth in what you said," he admitted, trying to crawl out. "He *has* fought for America. And I'm willing to do the right thing by him."

"You will?" yelled Uncle Henry, wheeling close to him.

"If I get this place, I'm willing to give him a good bonus," Hardy continued.

Uncle Henry leaned forward, all eagerness. "How much?" he cried.

"Say, five hundred dollars," the loan shark generously offered.

"I knew there was a ketch in it!" Uncle Henry said, and rolled back in the shadows of the alcove.

Lopez had been listening intently. Now he stepped up to Hardy and said: "Senor Santy Claus, now I understand why it is so 'ard for your country to get ze soldier. In Mexico, ze soldiers would take all ze money and give ze people a bonus... per'aps." He puffed his cigarette. "I am done wiz you." He turned abruptly to Lucia. "Now I shall come to you."

She started.

"You love my frand, Senor Jones?"

Gilbert intervened. He could not stand this. "I don't know what you're getting at," he said to Lopez, "nor how you're going to get it. But you must see that you can't discuss a thing like this here. It's impossible - utterly impossible." He was suffering vicariously for Lucia.

Pell sneered. "Your delicacy is somewhat delayed," he murmured.

"I don't mind business discussions. But there's been too much insinuation to-day. I won't have any more of it," Jones said.

Lopez looked affectionately at the young fellow, "But if I would make you 'appy...." he said.

"I don't want to be made happy at a cost so great," Gilbert affirmed.

Lucia's lovely head drooped, and she moved to the window.

"It shall be but a moment," the bandit promised. Gilbert walked to the fireplace so that his face would not be seen. Lopez went over to Lucia. "Senora, you do not wish to speak of love. Why?"

"I am married," was the answer.

"And because you are marry, you cannot speak of love?...Eet is strange customs. Tell me, senora, what does your marriage service say?"

"One promises to love, honor, and obey, in sickness and in health, till death shall part."

Lopez smiled. "All zat you promise?"

"Yes," very low.

"And yet you 'ave divorce!"

"Yes," lower still.

"So zat, after 'aving promise to love, honor, and hobey," he tapped off one finger at a time, and looked as if he wanted to get this mysterious matter straight in his mind, "until death, you 'ave ze right to break your word because ze judge say you can? Is zat it?"

"Y-y-y-yes. I suppose so."

Lopez smoked a moment, looked at the ceiling, and then said, "Well, why not break it yourself and save ze trouble!"

"It's the law," Lucia told him.

"Humph! An' what does ze 'usband promise? An' 'as 'e kept 'is promise?" There was no reply. "Is plain 'e 'as not. Zen why should you keep your word to 'im, when 'e 'as broken 'is word to you? Eh? Why do you not go before ze judge and 'ave your promise broken? Why ees it ze custom of your country? Why? Why?" He looked bewildered.

Lucia could say nothing. What was there to say? Suddenly Uncle Henry's sharp voice was heard: "I'll tell you why!"

Lopez turned to him. "And why?"

"She ain't got no money," Uncle Henry informed the room.

Lucia lifted her face. "Oh, do you think that would make any difference?"

"So!" Lopez was interested, "'Er 'usband? 'E 'as money?"

"He's richer'n mud," Uncle Henry declared.

Pell started to speak; but Pedro stopped him by lifting his gun.

"How much?" Lopez asked, not noticing.

Uncle Henry was bursting with information. "He's worth millions, the big bum!"

The bandit's eyes opened wide. "Millions!" he repeated. He looked at Lucia. "Yet 'e give nozzing to ze wife. H'm! Senora, tell me....Does a widow in your country get any of 'er 'usband's money when 'e dies?"

Pell, listening intently, drew a sharp breath. He caught the significance of the question. His lips contracted. This damned bandit was capable of anything.

Lopez paid no attention to him. He asked for enlightenment from Hardy. "Senor Loan Fish, do you know?"

Pell ventured to get out part of a sentence. "Say, what the..." But Pedro's active gun came against his ribs, and he paused, as who would not?

"She gets it all - the wife," Hardy told Lopez. "That is, if the husband hasn't made a will."

"'Ave you?" the bandit turned on Pell. "'Ave you made a will?" His tone was incisive. "Do not lie."

"No, damn you!" Pell in his rage cried out. "But I'm going to, the first min -"

"Good!" smiled Lopez.

Pell was puzzled, "What do you mean...good?"

Lopez did not answer him; instead, he addressed Lucia: "Senora, your 'usband 'e is bad frand for you. 'E beat you, sometimes?"

Lucia was startled. "Why do you think that?" she asked.

"I 'ave known ladies what are beaten. It is in ze eyes ... as in dogs and 'orses." He waited a second before he went on, came close to her, and peered earnestly into her eyes. "*Si*, I sink your 'usband a evil man." He turned on Pell again. "Say, who are you? Your business, I mean?"

"I'm in Wall Street," Pell said, in a low voice. What in God's name was this bandit going to do? What was his game?

"Wall Street? 'Aven't you never done anything honest? You go to ze war, per'aps, like my frand, Senor Jones?"

"I was in Washington," Pell winced. "A dollar-a-year man."

"You use your money, your power, to escape ze war? So! You are not only a skindler, but a coward. While my frand fight, you stay to home, to torture ze woman, H'm! I see it all now. Nice boy, you!"

Pell could scarcely articulate now, but he managed to get out, "By God, I've had enough of this - just about enough!"

Lopez looked at him coldly, a glint in his eye that should have warned Pell. "Do not worry," he said. "You are about through." He turned to his friend, Gilbert. "And now, my frand, you shall go." Young Jones did not understand him.

"Go?" he asked. "What do you mean?"

Lopez looked at him calmly, "I 'ave much business to do. You shall not 'ear, nor see, because for you is love, romance! Not business, which are soddid. Leave all zat for me, which am a business man." He smiled upon Lucia. "As I said, life 'as been unkind to you, senora. Ze silly law...ze foolish custom...'ave been around your 'eart, around your soul, like chains. But fear no more," he assured her. "For I, your frand, shall make you also 'appy." He put his arm around her.

She was fearful of his plans. "What are you going to do?" she cried.

Lopez laughed. "Wait and see. Life shall be yours. And love! Planty money! All what your 'eart desire. Now go...."

Pedro started to show them out the door. Gilbert, seeing the movement, said:

"But I don't understand..."

"I shall call you soon," Lopez said. "Zen you shall see. Now go." He got between them, and affectionately directed them to the door.

Gilbert turned to him. "You aren't going to..."

The bandit smiled. "Do not worry. I shall do no 'arm. Only good. Please go, my frand."

Lucia and Gilbert, deeply puzzled, obeyed, and followed Pedro into the open air. What did this portend? There had been a strange look in the eyes of Pancho Lopez.

CHAPTER XI

WHEREIN A MAN PROVES HIMSELF A CRAVEN,
A SHOT RINGS OUT, AND THE BAD MAN
EXPLAINS ONE LITTLE HOUR

A heavy silence fell upon the men who were left in the room. The bandit, unconcerned, puffed his cigarette. Hardy and Pell felt like rats in a trap. Only Uncle Henry was passive. In the tense stillness, the clock could be heard ticking on and on. Pell was beginning to crack beneath the strain. Suddenly he began to pace the floor, his hands behind his back. No tiger in a cage was ever more impatient in his captivity.

"If you want money," he finally got out, "for heaven's sake, tell me how much, and..."

Lopez quickly interrupted him. His fury boiled over at the insinuation. "Be still!" he cried. "You will please be quiet. I 'ave business to sink out which are 'ard."

Pell was equally angry. "Why, damn you ..." he sputtered.

He should have known better. Coldly Lopez took him in. "I 'ave been patient wiz you - too patient. I see zat now." The other returned his keen gaze, and for an instant he did not quail; but finally he could stand the strain no longer. His eyes fell away, and for the first time in all their bitter encounter he felt himself sinking. A terrible uncertainty came over him.

Charles Hanson Towne

This Mexican, this beast, was going to do something desperate. There was not the shadow of a doubt about that. He must go carefully: he must not lose his self-control. To do so would be madness.

Luckily, Uncle Henry broke the tension just then: "Am I going to get my money back?" he cried out. And his chair projected itself into their midst.

Lopez faced Hardy, across the table. "Senor Loan Fish," he said, "if my frand, 'e pay you ze money, zen ze rancho belong to him?"

"If he pays me before eight o'clock," the other replied promptly.

"Senor Wall Street," the bandit now addressed Pell, "you 'ave ten sousand dollar. I want it."

Pell was amazed. "But I -"

Lopez snapped his fingers. Pedro, who came back at that very moment, took the money from Pell, and watched his master closely for further instructions as to what to do. Lopez nodded toward Smith.

"For 'im," he said.

"For me?" cried Uncle Henry, joyfully.

"I must make my frand 'appy," the bandit said. Pedro gave the money to Uncle Henry. The latter grabbed it as a child might have grabbed a cooky.

Lopez turned to Pell. "Now - you is rob." To Hardy he said: "You is paid," and to Uncle Henry, "An' you get your money back. *Bueno!* Ees finish."

Pell was cynical. "I'll say that's service," he murmured; and a sardonic grin came to his thin lips. Perhaps the bandit was joking, after all. But damn these jokes that kept one in long after school!

Uncle Henry, however, had a strange apprehension, and wheeled about, facing Lopez.

"You ain't goin' to take it back from me, are you?" he inquired.

"No, Ooncle Hennery," the bandit laughed, "she is yours for keeps. Zat is all. You may go!" And he waved him out. "And you," to Hardy. "Pedro, show zem into ze open space!"

"'Im too?" asked Pedro, indicating Morgan Pell who stood, as though made of stone, in one corner.

"*Poco tiempo!*" the bandit said.

"*Debommultalo!*" his henchman replied.

"*Si*," Lopez smiled. And Pedro got the invalid and the lanky Hardy through the door, as a woman might have swept two geese from her path.

Left alone with the bandit, Pell remarked:

"Look here, there must be some way to settle this thing." But he had grave fears.

"To zat, I 'ave come at last," the bandit replied with an emphasis that could not be mistaken.

"You have?" Pell's voice was weak.

"It shall cost me planty money. I could 'ave tooken you wiz me for ransom - 'elluva big ransom - a million dollar, mebbe. But I am not soddid!" He laughed, and rubbed his hands together.

"You aren't going to hold me for ransom?" Pell questioned, relief in his voice.

"No."

"What - what are you doing to do?"

The reply was as swift as an arrow. "Kill you."

Pell did not believe what he heard.

"Kill me?" he repeated, his head on one side, like a bird listening, and pointing to his chest.

"*Si.*" Lopez had never used a politer tone.

"You - you're joking." There was a crack in Pell's voice.

"Joking?"

"You must be!" huskily. "I thought so all along - now I'm sure of it."

The bandit faced him, and threw his cigarette over his shoulder in the chimney-place. "Do I look like a joker?"

"You sit there, like that, and talk of killing me in cold blood?"

Lopez took him in through half-closed lids. "I do not like you. Nobody like you. Alive, you are no good. Dead, you make two people which I love 'appy. You get me, Senor Wall Street?"

"Oh, I see," cried Pell, wildly, and doing his best to keep his legs from giving way, "you would kill me so that my wife can marry this Gilbert Jones?" A sickly smile curled around his mouth.

Lopez nodded. "*Si, senor.*"

"If that's all, I'll give her a divorce!"

"You weel give her a divorce?" Lopez repeated, pretending to be much interested and pleased.

Pell saw a gleam of hope through the darkness of this moment. "Yes," came breathlessly from him. "Then she can marry him. Don't you see? If that's all you want - he can have her." He was shaking now in every limb. Escape was almost his. He knew he could not be done away with. "I'll give her to him!" He staggered toward Lopez, "I will! I swear I will!" he screamed, his words reaching a high falsetto.

Lopez rose. "I would look at you once before I shoot," he said slowly, and took in the other's cringing form.

"What?" Pell said.

Disgust was on the features of the bandit - contempt and unbelievable loathing.

"I 'ave met mans which would not fight for zeir money," he said with great deliberation, his lip curled. "I 'ave met mans which would not fight for zeir lives. But I 'ave never before met ze man which would not fight for 'is woman."

Pell saw that he was doomed now. He made one final desperate attempt. "But if you - shoot me - you'll be hanged!"

"Ha!" laughed Lopez. "If I am ever caught, I shall be 'anged many times!"

"I'm an American citizen!" shrilled Pell.

"I 'ave kill many American citizens," replied Lopez, without the slightest compunction.

Pell wrung his hands. "My Goverment will pursue you!"

"You are mistaken. Your Government will watchfully wait. We kill American citizen. Your Government write us beautiful letter about it....But we have waste time!" He drew his gun.

As Lopez leveled the weapon. Pell all but dropped on his knees. "Wait!" he cried. "I'll give you money! Plenty of money! A million dollars! Yes, two million!" It could not be that so shameful a fate was to be his.

"It is not zat we want money," the bandit replied. "It is zat we *don't* want *you*."

Terror seized poor Pell. "But for God's sake," he wailed, "you wouldn't do that! You couldn't! Without even a chance for my life. At least fight me fair!" His voice seemed far away to him - like the voice of another being from a distant world.

"Fair?" Lopez rolled the word over.

"Give me a gun, too!" the fool prayed.

"Give you a gun! Pedro!" The man had evidently been just outside the door, and came in at once. "Pedro, you 'ear?" And Pedro grinned.

"Yes! Give me a chance!"

"I shall never understand ze American idea. I give you a gun, you say?"

"Yes! That's the least you can do!" Pell was weeping now.

"But if I should give you a gun, you might shoot me wiz it!" Lopez laughed.

"You won't?"

"I am no damn fool!" the bandit cried. And he deliberately raised his gun again.

"You're not going to kill me? No! for the love of God, don't!" He plunged forward, groveling at Lopez's feet. A woman in a melodrama could not have begged harder for mercy. "Spare me!" were the words that fell from his pitiful lips. "For God's sake, spare me! I'll do anything! Go anywhere! He can have her! You can have her! Her, and all the money I've got, if only you'll spare my life!"

The bandit looked down in utter disgust at the cringing form. Never had he seen anything in the world that he detested more. Pell's fingers were on the bandit's boots.

"I did not know zat even a dog could be so yellow," he said. Then he turned to Pedro. "I do not 'unt rabbits. You kill 'im, Pedro." And he would not look again on the miserable specimen of a man that wallowed there on the floor.

"Ah! for the love of God!" came from Pell, who had half risen. At that instant Pedro shot from his hip at the debased creature. The form stiffened and collapsed like a bag, falling partially under the table.

"It is a good deed," said Lopez, turning. "He was evil man."

The shot had been heard without. "Red," Gilbert, Hardy, and a few Mexicans rushed in at the sound.

"Who shot?" cried the former.

"Pedro," said Lopez.

"But what was he shooting at?" "Red" asked.

Lopez smiled. "Only ze 'usband."

"What!" cried "Red." He turned and saw the body of Pell lying sprawled on the floor, and horror came over him. "You've killed him!" His voice was husky.

Charles Hanson Towne

"I 'ave. Most enjoyishly!" said Lopez, lighting a cigarette.

Gilbert went over and stared down at the mute frame. "He's dead," he announced. "Completely. Pedro never misses," was the bandit's only comment.

"But to kill a man - like that! In cold blood!" Hardy gasped. "Oh, it's horrible!"

"Why not?" Lopez wanted to know. "Ze skindler, ze coward what beat his wife. Was evil man." What white-livered folk these Americans were!

Gilbert looked down at Pell's body, which had now, in death, a certain curious dignity. "But don't you see what you've done?"

Lopez looked at him in bland amazement. "You wouldn't still fool around wiz ze foolish law, ze silly court?" he inquired. "Do you not see 'ow much better is my way? One hour ago you 'ave no money, no rancho, no woman. One little hour! Ze money she is paid, ze rancho she is yours, and ze woman what you want to marry is free for do so!" He looked Gilbert in the eyes, and came close to him. "Tell me, 'ave I not keep my promise? 'Ave I not make you, in one little hour, a 'appy man?"

CHAPTER XII

WHEREIN THE BAD MAN CANNOT UNDERSTAND THE GOOD MAN AND DISAPPEARS; AND A DEAD MAN STIRS

Immediately after, Lucia came in. She saw the body of her husband, the legs drawn up a bit, the arms stretched out, the wounded head turned so that the blood flowing from the forehead could not be seen. Only a few moments before, this limp, pitiful object had been speaking to her - calling her by name. It seemed incredible that Pell was powerless now to harm her. Brute though he had been, he gained, in this awesome instant, a strange glory, as the dead always do. The splendor of that universal experience was suddenly his; and, even lying there like a discarded meal-sack, he took on something of the pomp of a cardinal who had died. Never, of course, had she respected him more; and though she could not bring herself to shed a tear, she looked down at the still body, huddled in a heap, and craved one more word with him. No matter what has happened between a man and a woman; no matter what tragic hours they have known, when the moment of separation comes, there is always that wish to have explained a little more, to have taken a different course in all one's previous actions. It was not that she blamed herself; she had nothing on her conscience. But there was an instinctive dread at meeting the certain pain of this crisis.

She could not believe that he had gone from her like this. She had read of people being blotted out in such fashion; but that

Fate should bear down upon her household, that the lightning should strike within the borders of her garden, seemed impossible. Like everyone else, she never dreamed that a great tragedy could come to her. Just as we never think of ourselves as meeting with a street accident, so she never thought of this catastrophe. Yet there he lay, the symbol of that inexorable terror that moves through the world.

She went over quietly to a chair near the table and sat down. She hid her face in her hands. She did not wish to see that silent form again; yet he had been her husband, and her place, she knew, was by his side, in death even more than in life. How the world had changed for her in this little hour!

She had come into the room just as Pancho was finishing his talk with Gilbert; and she caught the force of his words. Now she heard him saying something else.

"And now, what you say? You all 'appy, eh?"

Gilbert was still too dazed to understand. "You've killed him!" was all he could utter.

"I 'ave," the bandit answered. "You need not thank me. It was a great pleasure." Evidently he smiled; Lucia would not look up.

Gilbert paced the floor. "He's dead!" he kept repeating, as though to brand the truth upon his brain. "He's dead!" He paused once and stared down again at the body.

"He's dead, just as I say," Lopez stated. "Pedro never misses."

As though he had heard his name spoken, the ubiquitous Pedro ambled in, slowly, and with a bored expression upon his ugly countenance.

"Azcooze, my general," he said. His chief turned. "It is ze damn ranger. Zey is after us some more."

Lopez never turned a hair. Lucia heard him say: "It is time. I was agspectin' zem. Ze 'osses?"

"Zey are ready," Pedro informed him.

Pancho paused and considered a moment. "Zey come from ze souse, zose rangers?"

"*Si,*" was the quick answer.

Lopez rose. "Felipe Aguilaw becomes more hefficient hevery day. I shall make general of 'im yet. *Bueno,* we go."

"Red" had gone over and looked out of the window. Twilight had definitely come, and the sky was a great sheet of flame. Orange, pink, purple, and red, the clouds shifted over the face of the dying sun. A king going down to his death could not have passed in greater glory. While men and women fought their little battles, waged their puny quarrels, this stately miracle occurred once more. Unmindful of the grief of mortals, the day was about to pass into the arms of the waiting night.

"What's it all about?" "Red" asked, turning from the wonderful scene without to the frightened people within.

"It is ze ranger what chase me some more again," smiled Lopez. He seemed wholly unconcerned.

"Texas rangers after you?" asked "Red," startled.

"*Si!*" laughed Lopez.

"And you don't even get excited?"

"For why? It is not my habit. I give not a damn for any man." He snapped his fingers, as though at life itself.

Two horses could be seen through the door. The men were

bringing them up to their leader. "We should take our time - is no hurry." He took his big sombrero from the peg where he had put it long ago, and turned to Gilbert. "Well, I go now. *Adios*, my frand."

"Wait a minute," the other tried to detain him. "You've killed him. You wouldn't go and leave things this way, would you?"

"As I say, no trouble for me," Lopez boyishly said, and smiled, shrugging his broad shoulders.

Gilbert was astonished. "Yes; but how about me?" he wanted to know, "You do not think of that."

The bandit turned, amazed. "What ze matter? Are you not satisfied? You all what you say: zit - zot - zet!" He pinched his fingers, and made a funny little noise.

"I can't think," said Gilbert, sitting down, one hand on his forehead. "It's all so strange, so confusing to me. The world seems to be rocking beneath my feet. What does it all mean - this life we live for so brief a time? What does anything mean?"

Lopez came over to him and put his hand on his shoulder affectionately. "You Americanos so queer," he said, "For why you waste time thinking? Are you not rich? 'Ave you not ze beautiful lady to love like 'ell yourself personal?"

Gilbert jumped up. He thought he would go mad if this sort of thing kept up. "Good God, man!" he cried. "After what you've done, you can talk like that?"

"What have I done?" inquired the bandit, blandly. "Well, *what* I done?"

Gilbert looked at him in amazement. "You killed him! That's all."

Lopez smiled. "Sure!" He let the word loiter on his tongue. He pulled it out like so much molasses candy. "I killed him - sure. Was in ze way. What else could I do?"

"You've put a barrier between us. We're of a different brand, a different calibre. Don't you see?"

"Ees no way for pliz you. If I do not kill ze 'usband, ees all wrong. If I do kill ze 'usband, ees all wrong. Say," he looked at him in confusion, "what ze 'ell shall I do wiz ze damn 'usband, anyway?" He puckered his brow.

"Oh, I don't know," Gilbert said in desperation. What was the use in arguing with this barbarian? Yes, he was a barbarian - nothing else. They were miles apart. Centuries of belief and training separated them.

"You don't know?" Lopez said. "Pretty soon you find out. It surprise you now. But pretty damn soon when all shall go and leave you alone wiz 'er, you shall be sensible, too - like Mexican. To live is more strong as law. Wait and see, my frand, wait and see!" He shook his head mysteriously.

Pedro stepped forward. "Here is a pistol," he said to his master in Spanish.

Lopez looked at him. "Ah, *gratia*, Pedro!" He took the weapon from him and patted him on the back. Then he whispered something in his ear, handed it back, and Pedro gave it to Gilbert.

"Ze ranger. Zey come," he said as he did so.

"*Bueno.* I go," said Lopez, and started toward the door. Then he turned to Gilbert. "*Astuavago adios.* Maybe we will meet again, maybe no. *Quien sabe?*" He waved his hand, gave one last look at Pell's limp form, and cried, "*Adios!*" He was gone - vanished like a ghost.

They all were mute in the little room. They heard the hoof

beats of the horses as they galloped away. Fainter and fainter grew the sound. Then silence. And meanwhile the great night was falling like a curtain around them all. Through the doorway came the last beautiful beams of the sun. The mountains were like giant sentinels, row on row, unbelievably near in the semi-darkness. Far off, now and then, a bird could be heard calling. Soon darkness would envelop the earth, and this day of doom would be gone forever. Never might they see Pancho Lopez again. Gilbert would go north; and Lucia - He could not think.

Hardy broke the silence. He came over and looked down at Pell. "We can't touch him till the coroner gits here," he said grimly. There were, as always, ghastly details to be attended to.

"But I better make sure," said "Red," kneeling beside the body. "Right in the head. Not a chance." He was peering down at the gaunt face. "No, not a chance when you get it there."

Angela, hearing something outside, had rushed to the door and looked into the growing darkness. "I thought - What was that?" she exclaimed.

They all listened. Far off a shot could be heard - then another. But it must have been miles away.

"Red" sprang up. "Rangers!" he cried. "They're shooting!"

"Where are they?" Hardy asked.

"In the arroyo," "Red" replied. He was at the window, looking out. "You'll see 'em in a minute."

The sound of shots came nearer. It was as though a miniature army were storming the section near the adobe.

Uncle Henry, sitting in the alcove, was terrified. "What's that?" came his piercing voice.

"They see him!" cried "Red."

"Do you think they can hit him?" Angela cried.

"Red" was certain they could not. "There ain't a chance, at that range," he said.

But Uncle Henry was not so sure. "Mebbe they might, by accident."

"Red" turned. "Accidents don't happen in Arizona - leastwise not with guns."

The horses' hoof beats came nearer. Yet in all the excitement, Lucia did not move. She was keeping her silent place by the body of Morgan Pell. She did not even raise her head.

"Here they come!" cried Angela, leaning out the doorway.

"Red" had gone out of the room; but he came back now. "Better get inside," he warned them all, definite fear in his voice. "We're in range. It's pretty dangerous. As I said, accidents don't happen down in this country."

"But I want to see!" cried Angela, dancing with excitement now.

"Red" was distracted. "Please come in, Angela," he begged. More shots were heard. He was frightened for everyone. He had lived too long down here not to know the meaning of such desperate shooting. "What the h -" Two bullets came through the window, and smashed a little mirror that hung on the wall near the staircase. The bits of glass fell to the floor with a loud crash.

"What's the matter?" came the terrified voice of Uncle Henry. His hands clung to the wheels of his chair. But he did not budge it.

Charles Hanson Towne

"Red" had not been able to dodge a shot. "Right through the hat!" he cried, and waved his Stetson. Sure enough, a bullet had gone clean through his headgear. Had he lifted his face a few inches higher, he would have been shot himself.

More hoof beats. Yet Lucia never moved.

"Bullet?" asked Hardy.

"Yes," "Red" replied. "And it was spang new - this hat. Cost eighteen dollars!" He was still looking at the tattered Stetson.

"Oh, it might have hit you!" Angela cried and embraced him.

"Told you we'd better keep inside!" "Red" said.

"You bet - until they go by," Hardy agreed.

"Red" stepped forward. "Back, everybody!" he ordered. He pushed everyone farther back into the room, until they were all crowded in one corner. Uncle Henry was trembling like a leaf. How he wished he had never been brought to this strange country! Oh, for the peace of Bangor, Maine! *There* was a place for you! Down here it was all shooting, killing, and desperate trouble. Having escaped one crisis, was it possible the fates were to be so unkind as to put him in the way of another, from which there might be no extrication? Curse the luck, anyhow. Gol darn it!

The hoof beats came nearer and nearer. There were more shots. A man dismounted near the door. Then a man on horseback galloped up to the very entrance of the adobe. There was a general movement without, but no one ventured to go out and see what had happened. They could hear voices, sharp commands, and far off one more shot. Someone cried, "Keep on after him, boys!"

A ranger came in. He was an angular fellow, with a bushy mustache, and eyes like a ferret. His gun was on his hip, and one hand never left it. His name was Bradley. Gilbert knew him well. Often had he met him in the hills. He was known as one of the best shots of all that company of men who pursued criminals and bandits through the State, and drove them over the border. Few escaped him; and he had a train of lieutenants who adored him. A born fighter, a born pursuer of men, who loved his desperate life, and gloried in his conquests. Some called him Bradley the Inexorable. He seldom missed a shot; and God help those who came into his power.

"We're after Lopez," he said breathlessly. "Been here?" He never wasted words.

"Yes," Hardy answered. He looked toward Pell's body.

Bradley's quick eyes followed his. "Hello! what's that? Wounded?" he asked.

"Worse - he's dead," Hardy replied.

Bradley stepped close to the still form. "Who did this? Lopez?"

"Yes," from Hardy.

"Got it in the head, eh?" the ranger went on, looking down at Pell, but with no pity in his face. He was too accustomed to death. A man who had been killed was just another "case" to him - one of an endless row of corpses.

Angela came up to the table. "He's really dead?" she breathed, and clung to "Red's" big arm.

"Who was he?" Bradley inquired.

Hardy motioned to the mute Lucia, sitting so quietly in the chair. "Her husband. Name's Pell."

"Sorry for you, lady," said Bradley, perfunctorily, as he might have said "Good-morning." He turned now to go. "Don't

Charles Hanson Towne

touch him till the coroner comes," he commanded. "Mind what I say."

"But officer - " began Hardy.

"Can't stop," Bradley waved him aside. "Now we *gotter* get him." He went out as swiftly as he had come in. Every instant was precious. There was not a second to be lost.

And still Lucia did not stir a muscle. It was as if she had been turned to stone. A silence fell upon them all. "Red" sat down on the little window-seat, his Angela beside him. Hardy tried to smoke. They could hear the clock ticking on and on - that little clock which had heard so much as its hands moved around the dial during the last few pregnant hours.

Suddenly Uncle Henry, who had been looking at Morgan Pell's huddled form, cried out;

"Hey, what's comin' off?" Had the darkness deceived him?

"Red" jumped at the question. "What's the matter?" His nerves were on edge.

"He moved!" cried Uncle Henry, excited now, and rising in his chair, which he wheeled out into the room.

"Moved!" cried "Red." "You're crazy! He's stone dead, if ever anyone was."

"I seen him - I swear I seen him!" Uncle Henry's eyes were almost popping from his head. "Why didn't someone do something? Why didn't they see what he saw? Oh, to be able to walk, and not sit forever like a dried mummy in this chair!

"But how could he have moved?" "Red" exclaimed. "He's dead, I say!"

"I don't know how he could!" Uncle Henry cried, "but he did!

Look at him!" He could scarcely control himself now.

"Maybe Lopez didn't kill him after all," "Red" said, and knelt down to examine Pell's body again.

"Now don't tell me that!" Uncle Henry yelled. "Ain't we got trouble enough here without him comin' back?" He could have stood any calamity, it seemed, but the return to life of this wretched Morgan Pell.

"By golly!" "Red" exclaimed, on his knees, his hand on Pell's white face.

"Was I right?" Uncle Henry said.

"Red" rose slowly. His voice was almost a whisper. "He's alive!" he breathed.

Gilbert, who had not taken Uncle Henry's word seriously, could not doubt "Red's" verdict.

"Alive!" he said. "Oh, it can't be!"

For the first time Lucia moved. Her lips opened. "Alive!" she managed to say. Again the world crumbled for her.

"It was only a flesh wound," "Red" said. "The bullet just grazed his head."

Lucia looked up. She was ashen. She was older, and her eyes seemed to have lost their fire. "He's - really - alive?" she got out. She stared down at her husband.

"They should of shot 'im in the stomach!" Uncle Henry stated. What a mess! What rotten luck, ran through his weary brain.

Pell's foot moved again. Then his arm went up; and slowly he rose on one elbow, pushed away the tablecloth that touched his head, and looked about him. He was like a man awaking

Charles Hanson Towne

from a sound slumber. He was dazed, mystified. In the almost complete darkness, he could not distinguish faces.

"What was it? What happened?" he inquired, in a hollow voice - a voice from the tomb!

No one answered. They were all terror-stricken.

"I can't remember," the hollow voice went on. He fell back on the floor. He was weak from the loss of blood. "Red" lifted him up, and helped him around the table to a chair.

Lucia's eyes never left Morgan Pell's face. Was she dreaming? Was this some madness that had come to her? This brute come back to life! It was unbearable, unbelievable. She could not adjust her mind to the situation. But with true feminine instinct, she found herself leaving her chair where she had sat so long, going to the kitchen and getting a cup of water. Then she knew, in some strange way, that she had fetched a bowl, and a towel. These she placed on the table. Still she looked at her husband, as though he were a ghost - as, literally, he was. They had thought him dead - gone forever. Now he was back among them, speaking, moving. Incredible! One hand went to her face. She dreaded the thought of Morgan's seeing her.

It was Uncle Henry who broke the awful tension.

"You was shot!" he cried, to Pell.

The other looked at the old man in the chair. "Shot?" he said.

"Yes, and a rotten shot it was, too!" Uncle Henry was not afraid to say. "Gol darn it all!"

The moment was too tragic for anyone to smile.

"Who shot me?" Pell asked. He was very weak. He put the towel in the bowl of water, and pressed it to his forehead.

"A friend of mine!" cried Uncle Henry.

Gilbert glared at the old man. No one could be forgiven for a remark like that.

"I remember, now," Pell murmured. "The bandit."

"And a gol darn nice fellow, too," Uncle Henry went on. "A little careless, but -"

Pell looked startled. The towel fell from his hand and he looked about him. "He's not here still!" he cried, as one just coming out of a stupor to a full realization of his surroundings.

"No, worse luck!" Uncle Henry said.

"He's gone?" Pell said.

"The rangers came," Hardy explained.

"Texas?" from Pell.

"Yes, gol darn 'em!" Uncle Henry let out.

Lucia, who had been watching Pell's face every second, now offered him the bowl of water with her own hands, and drew closer to him. She picked up the towel that had fallen to the table, and folded it, then dampened it. Pell looked up and saw her for the first time.

"Oh, so there you are, my dear!" was his cynical greeting.

Lucia still stared at him. "I thought - I thought - you were dead," she murmured. Her voice sounded far away to her. It was scarcely a whisper.

"So it seems!" Morgan Pell answered, his lip curling. "My dear, I regret to disappoint you. But aside from a slight pain in my head, I was never better in my whole life!" He wanted to see the effect of his words.

"Shall I bandage your wound for you?" his dutiful wife asked.

He looked at her from the corner of his eye. "Thank you - no," he said.

Lucia sat down on the other side of the table.

Not a word more was said. Pell took out his own handkerchief, and started to dip it in the bowl of water. But he was shaking still, and the piece of linen dropped to the floor. He stooped to pick it up. As he did so, he saw, in the dim light, the option lying exactly where Pancho Lopez had tossed it. He grasped it in his hand, crushed and crumpled as it was, and thought no one had observed him. But Uncle Henry's eagle eye had seen his movement.

"What's that?" he called out.

Pell tried to seem unconcerned. "The option, my dear sir," he answered truthfully.

"By gollies, he's got it again!" Uncle Henry yelled, in desperation. He switched his chair around, and faced Gilbert. "Why didn't you tear it up while he was dead?" he asked.

Pell addressed Uncle Henry. "You've got ten thousand dollars of my money," he firmly said.

"*I* have?"

"I want it," was the other's immediate reply.

"It was paid me for a debt," the old man said.

"It was stolen from me first," Morgan Pell stated, calmly. "Come across." He put one hand out. The other still held the cloth to his wounded forehead.

"I'll be cussed if I will!" the invalid cried. He clapped his hands over his vest pocket, where the money was safely hidden.

"Why, you poor old crook -" Pell began, rose, and snatched the money from Uncle Henry before anyone knew what he was doing. All his old fire was back. He seemed the most alive man in the room.

Uncle Henry cried out, wildly, "Hey, ain't there no Americans present?" He saw Gilbert's gun which was on the seat beneath the stairway. He was close enough to grasp it. He did so, pointed it at the room in general, and yelled, "Now I got yuh! Hands up, everybody!"

But no one moved. A disdainful silence followed. "Didn't yuh hear what I said?" Uncle Henry inquired, looking at everybody.

"Put that down," said Hardy contemptuously. "You might hurt somebody," he added, smiling.

"Ain't yuh goin' to do it?" Uncle Henry asked.

"As I was going to say -" Hardy started, when Uncle Henry interrupted him with:

"But it was what *he* done!"

"Who?" asked Hardy.

"The bandit," Uncle Henry answered.

"Will you keep still?" Hardy urged.

"Certainly not!" Uncle Henry went on. "I got a gun here and I -"

Hardy reached for the weapon. "I'm holdin' you up, gol darn it!" Jasper Hardy took the gun as he would have taken a bag of peanuts from a child, and handed it to Gilbert with a wink.

"Hey! You can't do that!" wailed the invalid. He wheeled his chair toward his nephew. "You wouldn't do that if my friend Lopez was here, you big bum!" he ended, as peevish as an infant.

Pell turned upon his wife. "Well, my dear -" he began, and once more his lips curled at the irony of the last phrase.

"What!" Lucia said; and there was terror in her voice.

Pell did not mince words. "Having both the Option and a clearer understanding of each other, there's nothing to detain us." He measured everything he uttered, and watched the effect upon her.

"It's no use," Hardy broke in. "You're too late."

"Not if I got there by eight o'clock," Pell said.

"But you won't!" Jasper Hardy quickly said, glancing at the clock which ticked on, inexorably.

Pell pulled out his watch. Then he looked at the option, deliberately, carefully, and seemed to read a final sentence. Having done so, he tore the piece of paper to bits slowly, and scattered them on the floor at his feet. At that very instant the clock struck eight.

"It's eight o'clock!" "Red" exclaimed on the last peal of the bell.

"Eight o'clock!" Hardy cried. "And the place belongs to me!" He turned to Pell. "Anything more from you?" he inquired, and smiled.

The other stared at him; but he said nothing. Instead, he went over again to the table, and wet his handkerchief in the bowl, again refusing Lucia's proffered assistance with a wave of his other hand. He bathed his own wound. And meanwhile Hardy was saying to Gilbert:

"Well, young feller, it's your move."

"His move!" "Red" repeated the phrase. "Say, you wouldn't go and skin him out of the place all over again, would you?"

Hardy sneered. "I'm going to foreclose, certainly, if that's what you mean, you impudent young scoundrel!"

"You mean you would trim him again?" "Red" didn't believe it.

"Say, boy, you better use your head. You're going to marry my darter, ain't you?"

"Yes - I hope so," the foreman said.

"Well, don't you realize that all I got will eventually go to you and her? Don't you?"

"It will?" asked the incredulous "Red."

"Certainly; when I die," answered Hardy.

"I hope it'll be soon!" cried out Uncle Henry. Then, to "Red," "Don't you see he's leading you up to the top o' that gol darn mountain?"

"Red" did not understand. "Gol darn *what*?" he said.

Uncle Henry was exasperated at his stupidity. "Why, he's temptin' you, the old devil! Don't let him. It's a gol darn shame," he added, turning his chair so that he faced Hardy, "an old scoundrel like you tryin' to corrupt a nice young feller like him! Don't you know money you get like that won't do you no good?"

"It's his - Gilbert Jones's," cried "Red," "and I ain't goin' to be party to robbin' him of it!"

"Hooray!" yelled Uncle Henry. "That's the boy! I knew you was like that. You're all right!" And he backed into the alcove, happier than he had been in a long time.

"You hear that?" Hardy said to his daughter.

"I do," she answered, "and he's right."

"What's that?" said her surprised father.

"It is Gil's, and to take advantage of him isn't fair. You know it as well as I do, too!" She stamped her little foot.

"Say, you don't think you love him again, do you?" Hardy wanted to know.

From the alcove, Uncle Henry cried: "That's the idea! And if the poor sucker'd only marry her -"

But Angela interrupted: "It isn't him I care for. It's -" She cut herself off, and could have bitten out her tongue for thus revealing her heart.

"Angela!" cried the enraptured "Red." He went over to her, grasped her around the waist, and led her to the window.

Hardy said, trying to pacify his daughter: "But I ain't going to be hard on him - or on Jones."

"You ain't?" Uncle Henry cried.

Hardy turned to the nephew. "You know, that stuff Lopez said about me bein' a bum patriot stuck in my craw. And now that I got the place, if you ever need any help I'll be glad to go on your note for you."

Gilbert said nothing; but Uncle Henry rushed in with, "You will?"

"That is, if it ain't too much," Hardy craftily added.

"How much?" Uncle Henry asked.

"Oh, two hundred dollars," Jasper Hardy grandly said.

"Two hundred dol - Git out o' my way!" Uncle Henry wheeled straight through him.

"Say, where are you goin'?" Hardy cried.

"To Mexico!" Uncle Henry said. "This country's gettin' so it ain't fit to live in!" And he whirled out of the room.

Hardy turned to his daughter. "Nothing to keep us here any longer. Come on, Angy."

"Come, 'Red,'" said the girl, as she started to follow her father. What else was there to do?

Even though it was Angela who called to him, "Red's" allegiance was for the moment elsewhere.

"I gotter stick by him," he said, looking at Gilbert.

"No," said Gilbert. "This is something I've got to settle alone. But I thank you, 'Red' - I thank you with all my heart. You're a brick - a red brick." He smiled and patted him on the back.

"Red" was suspicious still. He looked at Gilbert. "You don't think he'll try any funny business, do you? You're sure you won't need me around?"

"How can he try any funny business?" Gilbert asked.

"I know," said "Red." Gilbert looked at him closely. "I get

yuh," the foreman continued. "But I don't like it just the same." He switched over to the malignant Pell. "There's one little detail I'd like to call your attention to," he said.

"Well?" Pell said.

"I'm a tough little feller myself, sometimes. And if anything should happen that shouldn't, I'll be waitin' for you in town with a one-way ticket. And it won't be to New York. Savez?" Then he turned to his adored and adoring Angela. "Come, Angy!"

And he grasped her arm, and took her out.

CHAPTER XIII

WHEREIN AN OLD SITUATION SEEMS ABOUT TO BE REPEATED, ANOTHER SHOT IS FIRED, AND THE BAD MAN COMES BACK

Deeper and deeper grew the darkness. Outside, indeed, the first stars had begun to shine, and soon the heavens were a miraculous glory. But there was no moon. Every road was hushed, and the trees waved their long arms in the gloom. The little machine that took Angela and her father home, rolled down the quiet valley. Its chug-chug was the only sound for miles around. "Red" was happy in the cool night. He rode all the way out to the Hardy ranch. He and Angela sang an old song, and let Jasper Hardy sit at the wheel and whirl them to the lights of home.

Meantime, back in Gilbert's adobe, the Mexican cook came from his stuffy kitchen and fetched a lamp for the sitting-room. He lighted two candles by the fireplace, closed the shutters and door, and went back to his pots and pans. He said nothing, noticed nothing. It had been a day of intense excitement for him, and he was glad to crawl back, like some tiny worm, into the cave where he ruled supreme.

Lucia, in the lamplight, was paler than before. The three of them were standing, curiously enough, almost as they had stood only a few brief hours ago; and as she looked around her now she thought of this.

Charles Hanson Towne

"So," she said. "We're back just where we started from!" The grim humor of it came over her. Ten minutes ago she had thought her husband dead – done for, out of the way. Now he stood before her in all his virility, in all his cruelty; and behind him was the one man in the world that she loved.

"Not quite," said Gilbert. He stepped forward a pace or two. He saw that Lucia was alarmed. "Come," he begged of her. "Don't be afraid." Oh, the balm of those few words!

But she was not wholly herself yet. "What are you going to do?" she asked, and came nearer Gilbert. How strong and determined he looked in the dim light!

"I'm going to have this thing out," he said. "You can never go back to him now." There was finality in his voice.

"No, I never can," Lucia agreed. And there was finality in her voice, too. It was as if Destiny had come into this house, and an unheard voice told them what to do.

"You'll trust me to protect you - until -" Gilbert went on.

She looked at him pleadingly. "Oh, take me with you, Gil!" She threw her arms out. She had nothing to fear now, his strength beside her. She told him in one glorious gesture that she was his forever - that she had surrendered herself, body and soul, to him. Gilbert looked at her. Slowly, he realized that this woman, this creature of his dreams cared for him, and him alone; and the world might sweep by, the stars and moon might crash to earth, and they would neither know nor care. Fate had brought her to him. Nothing else mattered now. What was Morgan Pell? In life he was as impotent as when he lay half concealed beneath the table near which he now stood. They would not consider him, save as the foolish laws of man made it necessary for them to consider him.

Gilbert turned to Pell. "You heard - she's mine now. And any course you may take to stop her -" he warned. It was useless to say more. The manner in which young Jones spoke told the whole story of his feelings.

Yet Pell tried to appear nonchalant and casual. "You haven't another drink around, have you?" he inquired. He still held his handkerchief to his wounded forehead. "That was a rather nasty one I got, you know."

Gilbert, though he loathed him as a serpent, remembered that he was this creature's host, and stepped over to the fireplace where there was a flask with a little tequila still left. He offered Pell the bottle.

"You were saying -?" Pell went on. He poured himself a stiff drink. "Something about leaving me, wasn't it?" It was plain to be seen that he was bluffing. "I'm sorry," swigging down what he had poured, "but I wasn't listening very closely. This thing here - " he tapped his wound. No one answered him, and he set down his glass. "Well?" to his wife.

She faced him with a flame in her eyes. "Had I known you, I never would have married you. But now that I do know you, I could never live with you again. I loathe and despise you, with all the strength that is in me."

"You want to leave me, eh?" He sneered as he stared at her. "And go with him?...Won't your reputation - ?"

"What do I care for my reputation?" she flared. "At least I shall have my self-respect. I never could keep that if I went back to you."

"It's *your* reputation, of course," Pell smiled. "You can do as you like with it." He turned fully toward her. "All right, I've no objection."

"You're lying," Gilbert affirmed.

Pell's tongue rolled round in his cheek. "I don't blame you for

Charles Hanson Towne

thinking so. *You* haven't been shot to-day. You should try it sometime. It changes one's viewpoint surprisingly." His voice seemed to lose its hardness for a moment; there was a note of self-pity in it.

"But you said -" Gilbert began.

Pell's whole manner changed, and the look of a wounded animal came into his eyes. "A man says many things in anger that he doesn't mean," was his own extenuation. "Haven't you ever made the same mistake yourself, Jones? I'm sure you have. There's no use getting excited." He put up a hand. "Here we are, we three. She is my wife. But she doesn't love me, nor do I love her. She does love you. What is the best way out for all of us?"

A new Morgan Pell! They could scarcely believe the metamorphosis.

"You'd give her up?" Gilbert said.

The other looked down, and the point of his boot drew a little ring on the floor. "I can't hold her," he said, "if she doesn't want to be held, can I?"

"You don't intend -"

"To fight you?" Pell looked him squarely in the eye. "I do not. I've had all the fighting I want for one day. Now, my own course is simple. I have merely to go back to New York and forget that either of you ever existed. But your problem is more difficult. It's after eight. You've lost the ranch. And you have no money."

"But I can earn money," Gilbert said.

"A hundred dollars a month punching cows? With her in a boarding-house in Bisbee? A nice life, isn't it? Do you care to think of it, both of you?"

"I can take care of her," Gilbert was quick in saying.

"With your friend, Lopez - if he escapes - become a professional killer. My dear chap, you forget. She's used to decent people. It makes all the difference in the world." Pell turned away, lest the hard look should return to his countenance.

Lucia had been listening intently. "I know him, Gil," she whispered, loud enough for her husband to hear. "He's trying to frighten us!"

Pell faced her. "Frighten you? You're wrong, my dear. I'm merely trying to help you. That's all."

There was a step on the path - another step. Several people were approaching the adobe. Without ceremony, the door was thrust open, and Bradley was before them, excitement in his eyes. He came into the room and dim figures could be seen behind him. Was that Lopez tied up, with his back to them in the darkness? His shoulders were bent over, his hat was pulled down over his brow. His hair was matted, and two Mexicans stood guard on either side of him. Far away the stars twinkled, unmindful of his plight.

"Got any water?" Bradley asked.

"Lopez!" Pell exclaimed.

"He's got him!" came from Gilbert.

Lucia grew paler still. "Lopez! Captured!" she cried. "Oh!" And she hid her face in her hands. What a few brief hours could bring!

Bradley came close to her. "And a fine day's work for us, lady," he said, triumph in his tone. "We got him at last." Then, in the light of the candle, he caught a good view of Pell. "Say, I thought you was dead!" he cried.

"I was," laughed the other. "I mean - only a scalp wound."
And he pointed to the mark on his forehead.

The figure at the door, piteous in its helplessness, never
moved, never turned.

"Give me that water," Bradley continued. "I want to get him
in alive if I can. All the more credit to me and my men, you
see."

Morgan Pell had taken the canteen down from the wall and
poured some water in it. Now he handed it to Bradley. "There
you are," he said.

"Thanks," the ranger said. He went back to the door, and
pushed the jug to the lips of his prisoner. "Take a swig o' that."
Lopez did so. His humiliation was evident even in his back.
And only a little while ago he had been the monarch of all he
surveyed! Now he was the slave of Bradley, and must ride,
hand-cuffed, to the jail a few miles away.

"He's wounded," said Lucia, going to the door. "You can't
take him - like that!" she exclaimed. She longed for Lopez to
turn and look at her; yet she longed, oddly enough, that he
would not do so in the next second. It would be as difficult for
her, as for him, if they saw each other. Her heart went out to
him - this friend of Gilbert's - and hers.

Bradley hated this show of feminine weakness. "Why can't I
take him like that? Do you think I'm going to nurse an invalid
like him around these parts?" He took the canteen from one of
his men. "Here," he said, handing it back to Pell.

"That's all right. Keep it; you may need it later on," said Pell,
as though the jug were his to give away.

"Much obliged," the ranger thanked him, nothing loath.
"Come on, Bloke. Good-night. We got him!"

He gave the bandit a shove, and two other rangers grasped him by either arm. In a twinkling they were gone, had mounted their horses and were galloping away in the starlight.

So everything was over and done with! Lucia was heart-broken for Lopez. She came back into the room, murmuring:

"Lopez! Lopez captured!" There were tears in her eyes.

Pell paced the room with new strength. His eyes were now sinister.

"Fortunately for us, my dear," he said. "For now we are certain not to be disturbed while working out a sensible solution of our little problem." He had forgotten the pain in his head. He lighted a cigarette, casually, slowly. "You will of course sue for divorce," he went on, blowing a ring to the ceiling and watching it ascend. "But there'll be no difficulty about that. I shall not contest," he added magnanimously.

She grasped at the straw. "You won't?" She almost believed him now.

"You'd win, anyway," her husband said. "But there *is* the question of alimony."

Gilbert swerved about. He detested the word. "Alimony!" he cried.

"An attractive woman never gets the worst of it in court," Pell coldly stated. "Suppose we settle that - right here and now. It will give you ready money. And it will save me from having to pay perhaps a greater sum - later. That is...."

Gilbert was incensed. "We don't want your money!" he cried. And Lucia treated the suggestion with the scorn it deserved.

Pell looked at them both. "No? Well, in that case, I suppose there's nothing more to be said."

Charles Hanson Towne

"And we are free to go?" Lucia cried, unbelieving.

Her husband puffed again. "Why not? I know I shan't stop you." Suddenly he dropped his cigarette, leaned heavily against the table, swayed a bit, and put his hand to his head. The old pain was returning.

"You're suffering?" Lucia asked, alarmed. A strange pallor had come over him.

"I regret - that water - I gave away so liberally," Pell said, his voice weak.

"There's more," Gilbert cried. "I'll get it." He went hurriedly to the kitchen.

"Is there anything I can do for you?" Lucia asked, sympathy in her tone. Always with her was the womanly instinct to serve, to help. Morgan was like a wounded animal to her, and as deserving of attention as any hurt thing.

"No, thank you," he said.

"Oh, I'm sorry! I..."

Gilbert was back with another canteen. He went close to Pell and put the jug to his lips, standing by his side, leaning over to proffer the cooling water. As he did so, Pell stealthily reached out - Lucia could not see the movement, for she had gone over to the fireplace - and craftily removed Gilbert's gun from his hip-pocket. While in the very act of taking this man's sustenance, he was playing him a foul trick. His heart lost a beat at the easy success of his plan, the fulfillment of a wish he had been harboring for the last ten minutes. He thrust the canteen away, stood up suddenly, and pointed the stolen weapon straight at Jones.

"Now, I've got you just where I want you!" he snarled.

Lucia saw his base trickery. Why had she been so stupid as to believe in him again? Why had she not warned Gilbert? What fools they had both been!

"Gil!" she cried out; and anguish was hers - a deep, horrible moment of suffering. It was all up with them. They were as helpless as Pell had been with the bandit a few hours before. Caught, ensnared, trapped!

"Why, damn you!" Gilbert screamed, and made a futile lunge for Pell. But he was too late. The revolver was leveled at his head.

"Make a fool out of me, will you, you s -" Pell said, and his eyes glittered. A snake never looked more venomous. "I've got you now - got you both, and by God -"

"He means it, Gil!" Lucia cried, and threw herself into her lover's arms. She would die, if he died - she would die with him.

Pell stepped nearer to his intended victim. "Our wife is right," he scoffed. "It isn't killing that I mind - it's being killed that I object to."

"They'll hang you!" Gilbert warned.

Pell smiled his sardonic, evil smile. "The unwritten law works in Arizona as well as in other places." He brutally ordered Lucia to get out of his way.

But Lucia still clung to Gilbert. "I won't! I won't move!" she yelled, and her voice held the desperation of womankind.

Deliberately Pell said: "All right! Then take what's coming to you and you go to hell together, damn you both!"

He raised the gun and aimed a deadly aim.

Gilbert, in that mad moment, threw Lucia aside, to save her. He could not let her die with him, much as he hated to leave her with this fiend incarnate. "You'd better shoot straight," he cried to Pell. "Because, by God, if you miss...." With one wild lunge, he knocked the lamp from the table between them, and there was instant and terrible darkness.

Confused, Pell did not know what to do. His tongue was cleaving to the roof of his mouth, his hand seemed to freeze on the trigger.

"What the devil!" he called out. And then a figure appeared miraculously in the alcove, where one candle still burned, shedding a ghostly beam of light from a shelf. "Good God!"

A shot rang out. But it was not Pell's revolver from which it sped. Morgan Pell crumpled at the feet of Gilbert, and the bandit rushed in, the smoke still coming from his gun.

"Santa Maria del Rio de Guadaloupe!" he cried. "'Ow many time I got for to kill you to-day, any'ow? Now, damn to 'ell, mebbe you stay dead a while, eh?" He looked down at the shriveled form. And as of old he called to his henchman, "Pedro!"

And Pedro was there. "*Si!*" he said.

"Did I not tell you for kill zis man?" said Lopez, pointing in disgust to Morgan Pell.

Swiftly in Spanish, and frightened almost out of his wits, poor Pedro muttered something wholly unintelligible.

"Ees bum shooting! If she 'appen some more, zen I 'ave for get new Pedro. Should be too bad. Especially for you. You onnerstand?"

Terrified at the thought, poor Pedro simply shivered. "*Si*," he whispered.

Lopez indicated Pell's body, and took out a cigarette nonchalantly. "Take 'im away. Ees no use for nobody no more." Pedro started to lift the heavy form. "Save ze clothes and ze boots," he reminded his faithful man.

"*Si,*" the latter said, meekly.

Venustiano appeared from the outer darkness, as if by magic, and rushed to Pedro's aid. They lifted the stricken Pell, and carried him away.

The distasteful business finished, Lopez turned to Gilbert.

"Now, zen, you all right some more, eh?" he asked.

Gilbert could not understand. "I guess so," he said, "I - I thought you were captured!"

"Me?" said Lopez in surprise, "It is not me, ees my double!"

"Your double?" Gilbert, amazed, answered.

"Ees idea what I get from ze moving pitchers."

Gilbert and Lucia stared at each other; then at the bandit.

"Then it wasn't you they captured?" Gilbert said.

He flicked the ashes from his cigarette. "I should be capture by ze damn ranger? Ees a idea!" He roared with mirth. "No, no! Long time I 'ave fix zat."

"But how? How do you work it?" Gilbert inquired, his brain in a tumult.

"I pick from my men ze best rider. I make 'im for look like me. So when ze ranger wish for chase me, 'e go while I remain be'ind. It save me moch hexercise. Say, why you no kill 'im yourself? You got ze gun." Lopez was mystified.

Charles Hanson Towne

"I - I couldn't," Gilbert answered.

"Ees no difference from us three - me, you, and 'im," Lopez explained. "You is afraid for kill. 'E was afraid for die. Me, I am afraid for neizer! Now zen, what you do, eh?" He patted Gilbert on the shoulder.

"I don't know," the young man said. "We've got to go somewhere."

Lopez was firm. "No. You shall stay right 'ere in your 'ome sweet 'ome."

"But I've lost the place." He pointed to the little clock that was ticking out its relentless minutes. "It's after eight o'clock."

"No," said Lopez, definitely. "For at 'alf-past six-thirty, what I do? I tell you. When I am chase by ze ranger what I follow, I sink for myself eight o'clock she soon come. Suppose moggidge of my frands he meet wiz accident? Would never do!" He waved his arms. "So I goes and pays 'er myself!" He handed Gilbert a paper.

Gilbert could not believe his eyes. "What's that?" he wanted to know.

"Ees recipe," Lopez affirmed.

"But where did you get the money?" Gilbert asked, incredulously.

Lopez winked. "Ees all right."

"Where did you get it?" the American persisted.

"I rob ze bank," said Lopez; and thought nothing more of it.

"Robbed the bank?" Gilbert was wide-eyed now.

"Sure! Ees what I go to town for."

Jones turned away. "It's all off again!"

The bandit was discouraged. "No! I am become business man what are tired myself! I take ze money to lawyer what are frand for me. 'E go to ze judge what 'ave come 'ome planty dronk. 'E tell ze judge you send 'im for pay ze moggidge. Judge say sure, and 'and 'im recipe. Ees all right." And the bandit, convinced of his logic, strutted to the fireplace, and threw his cigarette away.

"But I - must pay him back," Gilbert wanted to make it clear.

"I 'ave planty money. You mus' not worry, my frand. I give you ten sousand dollar which you can send back should you be so foolish."

But Gilbert was obdurate. "I can pay it back. The oil -"

"I am sorry. Zere is no oil," the bandit informed him.

This was the consummating blow to the young man. "But you said -"

"I tell you one damn big lie," Lopez laughed. "But 'as she not a million dollar from ze 'usband which I kill?" He nodded toward Lucia.

"Oh!" cried she. "How can you speak of such things - now?"

"You don't think we'd touch one penny of that, do you?" Gilbert followed up.

Lopez looked puzzled. "Ze law is give it to you."

Disgustedly Gilbert cried, "The Law!"

"Ha!" The bandit saw his chance. "Is it possible all ze law what you love is not so damn wise, after all?" He was tickled at his own perspicacity. "However, it makes no never mind. You shall still be rich any'ow. I shall send back all ze cattle what I steal from you."

"You will? That's generous, to say the least." And Jones couldn't help smiling.

"And planty more what I shall steal for you myself personal. Now zen, is all right? You 'ave ze money, ze lady, everyzing." Surely there was nothing lacking, Lopez tried to make it plain, for complete happiness. There were no bars now in the path of content.

Yet this stupid young American was asking questions still! "But have I everything?" he said, and, stooping, picked up the gun that Pell had dropped just before he was killed.

Lopez was amazed. "Have you?" he said, and pointed to Lucia. "There is it!"

"But is it all right?" the young man persisted.

A look of scorn came over the face of the bandit. "If it makes you 'appy, what you care? You should not look ze gift 'appiness in ze face. Go on, take her. Ees nice; you like 'er."

Still Gilbert hesitated. "But I can't now."

"And why not?" the bandit asked. He was thoroughly weary of Gilbert's dilly-dallying, so foreign to his own philosophy.

"Maybe sometime. By and bye; but not now."

"If she is all right by and bye, why the 'ell is she all wrong now?" cried Lopez, incensed.

"You're not as sorry as I am. God knows, I want her."

Lopez was desperate by this time. "*Dios!*" he fairly yelled. "You Americanos make me seek! I shall come 'ere and work like 'ell all day to make you 'appy, and the best I get is zis!" In his despair, he broke into Spanish: "*Per dios mio!*" Stupidity could go no farther! What fools these youngsters were!

"I don't mean to be ungrateful," Gilbert explained.

There was silence for a moment. Lopez strode up and down the room like an animal. He was hot and disgusted. What was the use, after all? Why didn't this young fellow, who had proved himself so brave and so worthy, show signs of the red blood in him? No Mexican would have acted like this - no Latin. He would make him get his happiness, if he had to die in the attempt. Suddenly a crafty look came into his eyes. He came straight toward Gilbert and snapped his fingers in his face.

"Bah!" he cried.

But all the young ranchman said was, "I'm sorry. You don't understand our ways."

"Shut up!" Lopez was genuinely infuriated now. "Ees no use for talk wiz such fools. You make me seek! Such ideas! Not fit for ze child to 'ave! No blood, no courage! Only ze liver what are white and ze soul what are yellow." Gilbert winced at the word. "Americans! Bah! Fishes! Zat is all! Fishes what ees poor! Bah! For you I am finish!" And he snapped his fingers again. His face was purple with rage.

He heard Gilbert murmuring only, "I'm sorry!"

"Sorry! Ees all you can say - sorry! Ze coward! Ze fool! Ze fish what are poor! Ze damn doormat for everybody to walk from!" His arms were flying in the air. "All day I 'ave try to make ze man from you! It are no use. Ees no man in you. Only ze damn fool what are sorry! Bah! All right. You will not let me make you 'appy? *Bueno!* Zen I shall go back and make you on'appy and serve you damn good right!" He pointed to Lucia. "You will not take 'er?"

Gilbert had stood still during this tirade. "I've tried to explain - " he began once more.

"Bah!" cried Lopez. "Zen I take her!"

At last the American was roused. "You take her!" he cried.

"Sure! All day I 'ave want 'er. Ees ze first time in my life when I want woman all day and not - as favor I give 'er to you. Now, since you too big damn fool not to take 'er yourself, I take 'er myself. And what you know about 'im?" He paused, and called out, "Pedro!"

Fearful at what might happen, Gilbert said, "Wait a minute." He thought swiftly. "You mean this?"

Lopez did not even answer him, so deep and abiding was his disgust. Instead, he said to his man, "Pedro, we go."

Gilbert watched his every motion. "You mean it?" he repeated.

Lopez laughed. "Everybody sink I am joker to-day. Pedro, take 'er," and nodded toward the terrified Lucia.

Pedro started to obey.

"I'm damned if you do!" cried Gilbert. "All day you've been trying to make me do things your way. I've had enough. This Mexican stuff may be all right in your country, but it won't go here!"

He threw a protecting arm around Lucia, who was panting and pale. He pulled his gun, and aimed it at Pedro's head. "Drop it!" he cried. Pedro obeyed like lightning. The gun fell to the floor with a vibrating crash.

Then Gilbert covered Lopez. "If this is a trick -" he cried.

"Trick for what?" the bandit wanted to know. He nodded to Pedro. "Get ze men. 'E will not shoot!"

Enraged beyond control, young Jones cried out: "For the last time! You mean it? I know what you've tried to do, and I'm grateful; but there's one thing that I must do!" Still the gun was leveled at the bandit's head.

"What's that?" nonchalantly.

"Protect her!" Gilbert said, drawing Lucia closer to his heart.

Lopez smiled again. "You will not shoot."

"I will - if I must!"

"Oh, ze wolf in ze sheep's overcoat!" the bandit smirked.

"I will! I warn you!"

"Gil!" cried Lucia, in mortal terror.

"It's your life or his, and I'm damned if it's yours! I'll give you just three seconds to get out of here! Now," and there was a fire in his eyes that could deceive no one, "you hear me? One - two..."

"Don't shoot!" cried the bandit. And he laughed outright, almost doubling up with mirth.

"It was a trick?" Gilbert asked, beginning to see light.

"*Si.* Ah, my frand, I 'ave make ze man from you at last! Fine man what would kill for 'is woman!" He patted him on the shoulder.

Gilbert looked at him seriously, and the terrible realization came to him. "I *would* have killed you! Yes, I *would* have killed you - and you are my friend!"

Lopez saw how earnest he was. "I know. And it makes me very 'appy. For at last you 'ave became ze man of intelligence - like me. You could not leave 'er go now, could you?"

Gilbert looked at the relieved Lucia. "No!" he cried.

"You not question ze what you call Destiny, do you?" Lopez said.

"No."

"Zen for you I am Destiny, to beat 'ell!" He walked toward the door.

There was a whistle outside. Pedro had drifted into the night. The stars poured their miracle of beauty into the room as Pancho Lopez flung the door wide.

"Well, no more of zat!" he said. "I must go - to leave you to live and love! No, you shall not zank me," as Gilbert started to speak. "Ees I shall zank you, for 'ere in your quiet 'ome you 'ave give me ze most peaceful day I 'ave spend in years." He smiled his captivating smile, and for the first time took his sombrero from his head. He made a grand gesture. "Ees 'appy day for you. Ees 'appy day for 'er. Ees 'appy day for me!"

He made a very low bow. Then he stepped forward and touched Lucia on the arm, and led her to Gilbert. One hand was on the shoulder of each.

"You will name ze baby for me sometime - Pancho, or per'aps Panchita?" There was a wistful note in his deep voice, and a look of eagerness in his eyes. "Not ze first one, per'aps - but mebbe, like you say, by and bye - later? Eh?"

There was another whistle down the starlit road.

"*Adios*, my frands! And may you always be so 'appy like what I 'ave make you!"

He was gone. They heard the horses trotting away; and even in that moment of blinding and almost unendurable happiness, they were conscious of a tinge of sorrow.

For when would they ever see Pancho Lopez again?

CHAPTER XIV

WHEREIN AN OLD FRIEND RETURNS,
AND THERE IS A JOYFUL REUNION

On a wonderful afternoon, more than two years later, Lucia sat in the little Spanish courtyard that Gilbert had had built a few months after their marriage. The air was like golden wine, and she drank it in, bathed her soul in it, as though she could never find enough joy through these slow hours. How marvelous life had been to her in the last radiant months! She had realized the fulfillment of her most cherished dream, and looked down now at a tiny pink face that smiled at her.

"Oh, how sweet you are, Pancho!" she was saying. "I don't know what I ever did without you!" And she kissed the baby's cheek, which instantly took on a rosy hue.

There is an ecstasy that is close to tears; and in the happiness that Lucia had now found she was experiencing that high state of spiritual exaltation which made life almost unbearably beautiful. The autumn day itself, warm and glowing, was like a low fire on the hearth, toward which she stretched her hands. But there was a spiritual fire within her which needed no outward symbol; a flame that leaped and burned steadily.

Far off she heard the chug of a motor - not the Ford now, but a big touring-car that glistened in the sun. She knew that Gilbert would be returning from Bisbee at just about this hour, and she could hardly wait to see him turn in.

"Here's your daddy, Pancho!" she cried, when the car swung from the road, and Gilbert, hatless and sun-burned, leaped from the machine with all the eagerness of a great healthy boy.

He ran to his little family and kissed them both. "Gosh! but you look lovely, Lucia, my dear!" he exclaimed, standing back a bit so that he could have even a better view of her rosy cheeks, flashing eyes, and blowing hair. "This autumn weather agrees with you, doesn't it? And Pancho - he looks better than any baby around here - even Angela's."

He dropped down on the seat beside her, and looked with rapture at the child in her arms.

"Sold ten head of cattle this morning, and Montrose says he'll take as many more when I'm ready for him. Great, isn't it? 'Red' been over to-day?"

"Yes," answered Lucia; "and he said he was going to bring Angela and Panchita for an early supper. Says it's awful the way they've neglected us. We haven't seen them for two whole days, you know!"

They both laughed.

"Well, of course old 'Red' has more to do now that Jasper Hardy's dead; but after all, he can hire all the men he needs. Guess it's more a question of his wanting to stay around Angy and the kid, don't you think so?"

"He tries so hard to imitate you in everything. It makes me ache to see how happy he is, Gil. Aren't they the cutest couple you ever saw? And won't it be nice when Pancho and Panchita are old enough to play together?"

"You bet!" Gilbert agreed. He looked off at the quiet mountains, steadfast in their serenity, their crests seeming to kiss the sky. This *was* God's country, after all. Sometimes he could not believe that he had come so gloriously into his own.

In the slow process of putting his ranch on a paying basis, after the turmoil of those weeks following the departure of Lopez, he had had the sustaining wonder of Lucia always beside him; and when little Pancho came upon the scene he felt that life was altogether too kind to him. He had worked unremittingly; and not only had he had his own affairs to absorb him, but "Red," after his marriage to Angela, was forever ringing him up on the telephone, or coming over and asking his advice and help. He was never too busy to throw out a word to his faithful friend; indeed, they had reached a cooeperative basis so far as the two properties were concerned, and the arrangement could not have worked out better. The ranches touched each other, and after Jasper Hardy's death a year and a half before, it seemed wise to form a sort of partnership. There was no need of a written understanding; the two men simply said to each other that they would do certain things, install certain improvements, and share expenses and profits. Nothing on paper for them! No, siree, said "Red." He wouldn't hear of it. And everything had been as amicable as possible.

It was curious to see the change in Uncle Henry since the arrival of little Pancho. Gilbert got him a brand-new wheel chair - sent all the way to Phoenix for it - to celebrate the great event; and Uncle Henry loved nothing better than to take the chap on his knee and give him a ride in the courtyard whenever Lucia would trust him to his care. He never complained now. He was deliriously happy, and with the new era of prosperity that had struck the household, he was given a Mexican boy as his own personal attendant, and he grew to take a kindly interest in him. He taught him to read and write English. Thus busily occupied, and loving Lucia because she loved his nephew so, his health improved, as well as his temper. He could even tolerate "Red's" harmonica; in fact, he often begged him to play it when the latter came over to midday dinner, and his legs had so improved that he could actually jiggle them to some merry tune.

"If you don't look out, you'll be dancin' soon!" "Red" used to say on these happy occasions. "You can shimmy now!"

"Shet your head!" Uncle Henry cried; but not angrily - not now. He laughed when he said it, and was secretly flattered that anyone thought he had such pep at his age and in his condition of semi-invalidism (for that is all it could be called now).

It was five o'clock when the Giddings family came. They used the faithful little Ford for the short run; but they too had a big roadster, painted a flaming red, "to match the master's hair," Mrs. Quinn put it.

Angela, radiant in her motherhood, instantly compared notes with Lucia as to infant symptoms - not that anything was the matter with either child; but she loved to be ready for any emergency, and had a natural fear that Panchita might be taken ill in the night sometime; and was everything in her home medicine-chest, that should be?

Uncle Henry begged to take both children on his lap; and, holding them firmly, he made his boy push the chair here and there, got "Red" to play the once detested harmonica, and had a gay time of it all around the ranch house.

"We'd better eat indoors this afternoon," Lucia said. "I was going to spread the table under the pergola; but it may turn cooler."

It was not long before they were all seated at an extended table in the big living-room - that same room which had been the scene of tragedy and suffering for them, but was now so filled with joy.

"Mrs. Quinn sent over the cake," Lucia announced, as the table-boy brought in a huge dish, on which was a chocolate cake of magnificent proportions. It looked - and was - as light as a feather; a work of art to be proud of.

"Just like her, eh?" said "Red." "What would we do without Mrs. Quinn, the queen of 'em all!"

Charles Hanson Towne

"That's what I say," Uncle Henry declared. He could hardly wait to get to the cake, for he knew what toothsome dainties the Irishwoman could cause to emerge from her oven; and often she sent him this or that sweet, "just to let 'im know she was livin' an' breathin'."

Suddenly there came a sound of hoof beats on the road; and through the open door, outlined against the flaming sunset, Gilbert could see two horsemen approaching, with pointed hats, and glistening buttons.

"Mexicans!" he cried. "What can they be doing here, now?" His mind rushed back to that terrible evening so long ago when Lopez had ridden up to the adobe, and changed the world for them all in almost the twinkling of an eye.

He got up from the table now, and "Red" followed him. Dusk was just descending, but Gilbert's sharp eyes recognized the first horseman even in the dimming light.

"It's Pancho Lopez!" he cried.

And sure enough, on a steed that looked like Sunday afternoon, with brand-new reins and bit, and in a suit that fit him to perfection, with gleaming spurs and shining buttons, the rakish and indomitable Pancho, his long-lost friend, returned to greet him. He could scarcely believe it. For since that memorable night when he had left them, to return to the interior of Mexico, never a word had he had from him. Meantime, the great happiness had come to him; and when the baby came into the world, he and Lucia had not forgotten the man who had been responsible for their joy. With one accord they named the boy Pancho. There was not the slightest doubt but that should be what he should be called. The only tragedy was that they had no way of letting the bandit know what they had done. Where was he? They did not know. When, if ever, would he return? They had no way of finding out. There was but one thing to do - wait. And they did. But often Gilbert had said to Lucia, "He has forgotten us, though we have never forgotten him - our friend."

Now, in the quiet, brooding autumn dusk he came to their doorstep, dismounted, lifted his hat, smiled that wonderful smile of his, and made a bow that any courtier might have been proud to make. Behind him, on a brown horse, was Pedro, his lieutenant - the same monosyllabic Pedro, faithful unto death, and now as clean as a whistle.

"Ah! my frand!" Pancho said, as he bowed again, "How glad am I to see you. You glad to see me, too, eh?"

Lucia also had come to the door; likewise Angela - but the latter was still a bit timid. Even Uncle Henry pushed his way to the sill, and sat like a lonely man in a gallery while those in the orchestra pressed about their favorite actor.

"Glad?" exclaimed Gilbert. "I could kiss you, Pancho! But where on earth have you been? Come in, and tell us everything."

He needed no urging. "Hongry as beeg bear!" he told them.

"Then sit right down," Lucia said, "There's plenty - far more than the last time you were here!" And they all laughed.

He came into the room, while Pedro took care of the horses.

"Hallo, Oncle Hennery," he greeted the old man in the wheel chair. "You look splendid! And 'allo, 'Red,' - zat's what zey call you - yes?" Then he saw the babies, and his eyes fairly popped from his head, "Well, well!" he cried, "Who 'ave zese leetle fellers!"

"They're not both fellers!" Angela made bold to say. "One's a girl - that one! She's mine!"

"Oh, ho! Leetle spitfire still!" Pancho laughed. He chucked her under her pretty chin. "So you marry ze man I pick for you, eh? Good! An' zis" - pointing to the baby - "zis ees better yet!"

"Look at mine!" the proud Lucia couldn't help saying. "Isn't he the image of his father?"

She held him up, and Lopez took his little hand in his. "Yes, I see what you mean," he said, carefully looking at the child. "Hees father's eyes - but not so much hair! What you call heem?"

"Guess!" said Gilbert.

"Could not," the Mexican answered.

"Only one guess!" Lucia begged.

"Could not t'ink," Lopez insisted.

"Well, then - you tell him, Gilbert," the mother said, turning to her husband.

"There could be only one name in all the world for that youngster," Gilbert said, and put his hand affectionately on his old friend's shoulder. "You ought to know it as well as I. Of course his name is - Pancho!"

The smile that came over the Mexican's face was beautiful to see. And was that the suggestion of a tear in his eye?

Long and long, and while everybody in the room remained perfectly still, he looked at the baby, whose tiny hands bobbed up and down - a fat, healthy youngster, fit as a fiddle, laughing, squirming, happy.

"For me you name him?" Lopez finally got out. "Oh, too good you are to me. Pancho! my own leetle boy! Pancho! 'Some' name, what you say, eh?"

And he pinched the child's cheek, tenderly as his mother

would have done.

"And here's mine!" Angela, not to be outdone, piped up, presenting her child, also in her arms, to the delirious bandit.

"An' what heez name?"

"It ain't a he - it's a she, I told you!" Angela corrected.

"Ah! All kinds you 'ave 'ere, eh? Good! An' what *'er* name?"

"Can't you guess?" asked "Red," coming forward, smiling.

"A girl? What use I 'ave for girls?" laughed Pancho Lopez. "What you say now - what's ze name?"

"Why, Panchita! What else could we have named her?" Angela said.

You could have knocked the Mexican down with a straw. This time he was flabbergasted.

"You all too fine, too tender, too good to me," he said; and there was a softness in his speech that none of them had guessed could be there, save, perhaps, Gilbert.

"Oh, no," Jones said. "We wanted a little Mexican touch in our households. And we've never forgotten you, old friend. Tell me, where have you been all these months? We hoped to hear from you. But never a word or a sign from you. Aren't you just a little ashamed of yourself now, when you see how much we have been thinking of you?"

Lopez hung his head. "Yes, my frand, I *am* ashamed." Then he looked around at all of them. "I love you very much. I dream of you often, an' I say to myself. 'Some day I go back there, an' see my old frands which I make so 'appy.' But I bandit no more, an' travel I hate in trains. I reform. I settle down in Mexico City. I 'ave baby too, an' good wife, good mother. But

I get 'omesick, 'ow you say, for you all, an' so I come down for what you call 'oliday, an' - 'ere I am! You 'ave made me very 'appy to-night. I love you all even more seence I see zese cheeldrens. *Madre Dio!* How fine to 'ave cheeldren!"

"Ain't we ever goin' to finish our supper?" Uncle Henry wanted to know; but his tone was not querulous; it was plaintively sweet, and it held a note of invitation for everyone.

Laughing, they all sat down, but not before Pedro had been asked in. The frightened cook - the same who had been drunk that fatal evening when Pancho first arrived - scurried here and there, eager to serve the distinguished guest.

"You all right!" Lopez told him. "Never fear, so long as you bring me good 'ot coffee!"

And, happy as the babies, they all fell to; and it was Pancho himself who was asked to cut Mrs. Quinn's big cake.

"First time I use a knife in long while!" he laughed, as he stood up to the job. "Now we all eat much; an' mebbe give some to leetle Pancho and Panchita too, eh?"

Choose from Thousands of 1stWorldLibrary Classics By

Ada Leverson
Adolphus William Ward
Aesop
Agatha Christie
Alexander Aaronsohn
Alexander Kielland
Alexandre Dumas
Alfred Gatty
Alfred Ollivant
Alice Duer Miller
Alice Turner Curtis
Alice Dunbar
Ambrose Bierce
Amelia E. Barr
Andrew Lang
Andrew McFarland Davis
Andy Adams
Anna Sewell
Annie Besant
Annie Hamilton Donnell
Annie Payson Call
Annonaymous
Anton Chekhov
Arnold Bennett
Arthur Conan Doyle
Arthur M. Winfield
Arthur Ransome
Atticus
B.H. Baden-Powell
B. M. Bower
Baroness Emmuska Orczy
Baroness Orczy
Basil King
Bayard Taylor
Ben Macomber
Bertha Muzzy Bower
Bjornstjerne Bjornson
Booth Tarkington
Boyd Cable
Bram Stoker
C. Collodi
C. E. Orr
C. M. Ingleby
Carolyn Wells
Catherine Parr Traill
Charles A. Eastman
Charles Dickens
Charles Dudley Warner
Charles Farrar Browne

Charles Ives
Charles Kingsley
Charles Klein
Charles Lathrop Pack
Charles Whibley
Charles Willing Beale
Charlotte M. Braeme
Charlotte M. Yonge
Charlotte Perkins Stetson
Clair W. Hayes
Clarence Day Jr.
Clarence E. Mulford
Clemence Housman
Confucius
Cornelis DeWitt Wilcox
Cyril Burleigh
D. H. Lawrence
Daniel Defoe
David Garnett
Don Carlos Janes
Donald Keyhoe
Dorothy Kilner
Dougan Clark
Douglas Fairbanks
E. Nesbit
E.P.Roe
E. Phillips Oppenheim
Edgar Rice Burroughs
Edith Van Dyne
Edith Wharton
Edward J. O'Biren
Edward S. Ellis
Edwin L. Arnold
Eleanor Atkins
Eliot Gregory
Elizabeth Gaskell
Elizabeth McCracken
Elizabeth Von Arnim
Ellem Key
Emerson Hough
Emily Dickinson
Enid Bagnold
Enilor Macartney Lane
Erasmus W. Jones
Ernie Howard Pie
Ethel Turner
Ethel Watts Mumford
Eugenie Foa
Eugene Wood

Evelyn Everett-green
Everard Cotes
F. H. Cheley
F. J. Cross
Federick Austin Ogg
Ferdinand Ossendowski
Francis Bacon
Francis Darwin
Frances Hodgson Burnett
Frances Parkinson Keyes
Frank Gee Patchin
Frank Harris
Frank Jewett Mather
Frank L. Packard
Frank V. Webster
Frederic Stewart Isham
Frederick Trevor Hill
Frederick Winslow Taylor
Friedrich Kerst
Friedrich Nietzsche
Fyodor Dostoyevsky
G.A. Henty
G.K. Chesterton
Gabrielle E. Jackson
Garrett P. Serviss
Gaston Leroux
George Ade
Geroge Bernard Shaw
George Durston
George Ebers
George Eliot
George MacDonald
George Meredith
George Orwell
George Tucker
George W. Cable
George Wharton James
Gertrude Atherton
Grace E. King
Grace Gallatin
Grant Allen
Guillermo A. Sherwell
Gulielma Zollinger
Gustav Flaubert
H. A. Cody
H. B. Irving
H.C. Bailey
H. G. Wells
H. H. Munro

H. Irving Hancock
H. Rider Haggard
H. W. C. Davis
Hamilton Wright Mabie
Hans Christian Andersen
Harold Avery
Harold McGrath
Harriet Beecher Stowe
Harry Houidini
Helent Hunt Jackson
Helen Nicolay
Hendrik Conscience
Hendy David Thoreau
Henri Barbusse
Henrik Ibsen
Henry Adams
Henry Ford
Henry Frost
Henry James
Henry Jones Ford
Henry Seton Merriman
Henry W Longfellow
Herbert A. Giles
Herbert N. Casson
Herman Hesse
Homer
Honore De Balzac
Horace Walpole
Horatio Alger Jr.
Howard Pyle
Howard R. Garis
Hugh Lofting
Hugh Walpole
Humphry Ward
Ian Maclaren
Inez Haynes Gillmore
Irving Bacheller
Israel Abrahams
Ivan Turgenev
J.G.Austin
J. Henri Fabre
J. M. Barrie
J. Macdonald Oxley
J. S. Fletcher
J. S. Knowles
J. Storer Clouston
Jack London
Jacob Abbott
James Allen
James Andrews
James Baldwin

James DeMille
James Joyce
James Lane Allen
James Lane Allen
James Oliver Curwood
James Oppenheim
James Otis
James R. Driscoll
Jane Austen
Jens Peter Jacobsen
Jerome K. Jerome
John Burroughs
John Cournos
John F. Kennedy
John Gay
John Glasworthy
John Habberton
John Joy Bell
John Kendrick Bangs
John Milton
John Philip Sousa
Jonas Lauritz Idemil Lie
Jonathan Swift
Joseph A. Altsheler
Joseph Carey
Joseph Conrad
Joseph E. Badger Jr
Joseph Hergesheimer
Joseph Jacobs
Julian Hawthrone
Julies Vernes
Justin Huntly McCarthy
Kakuzo Okakura
Kenneth Grahame
Kenneth McGaffey
Kate Langley Bosher
Kate Langley Bosher
Katherine Cecil Thurston
Katherine Stokes
L. A. Abbot
L. T. Meade
L. Frank Baum
Latta Griswold
Laura Lee Hope
Laurence Housman
Leo Tolstoy
Leonid Andreyev
Lewis Carroll
Lilian Bell
Lloyd Osbourne
Louis Tracy

Louisa May Alcott
Lucy Fitch Perkins
Lucy Maud Montgomery
Lydia Miller Middleton
Lyndon Orr
M. Corvus
M. H. Adams
Margaret E. Sangster
Margaret Vandercook
Margret Penrose
Maria Edgeworth
Maria Thompson Daviess
Mariano Azuela
Marion Polk Angellotti
Mark Overton
Mark Twain
Mary Austin
Mary Catherine Crowley
Mary Cole
Mary Hastings Bradley
Mary Roberts Rinehart
Mary Rowlandson
M. Wollstonecraft Shelley
Maud Lindsay
Max Beerbohm
Myra Kelly
Nathaniel Hawthrone
Nicolo Machiavelli
O. F. Walton
Oscar Wilde
Owen Johnson
P.G. Wodehouse
Paul and Mabel Thorne
Paul G. Tomlinson
Paul Severing
Percy Brebner
Peter B. Kyne
Plato
R. Derby Holmes
R. L. Stevenson
R. S. Ball
Rabindranath Tagore
Rahul Alvares
Ralph Henry Barbour
Ralph Waldo Emmerson
Rene Descartes
Rex Beach
Rex E. Beach
Richard Harding Davis
Richard Jefferies
Richard Le Gallienne

Robert Barr
Robert Frost
Robert Gordon Anderson
Robert L. Drake
Robert Lansing
Robert Lynd
Robert Michael Ballantyne
Robert W. Chambers
Rosa Nouchette Carey
Rudyard Kipling
Samuel B. Allison
Samuel Hopkins Adams
Sarah Bernhardt
Selma Lagerlof
Sherwood Anderson
Sigmund Freud
Standish O'Grady
Stanley Weyman
Stella Benson
Stephen Crane
Stewart Edward White
Stijn Streuvels
Swami Abhedananda

Swami Parmananda
T. S. Ackland
T. S. Arthur
The Princess Der Ling
Thomas A. Janvier
Thomas A Kempis
Thomas Anderton
Thomas Bailey Aldrich
Thomas Bulfinch
Thomas De Quincey
Thomas H. Huxley
Thomas Hardy
Thomas More
Thornton W. Burgess
U. S. Grant
Valentine Williams
Various Authors
Victor Appleton
Virginia Woolf
Walter Camp
Walter Scott
Washington Irving
Wilbur Lawton

Wilkie Collins
Willa Cather
Willard F. Baker
William Dean Howells
William le Queux
W. Makepeace Thackeray
William W. Walter
Winston Churchill
Yei Theodora Ozaki
Yogi Ramacharaka
Young E. Allison
Zane Grey